Also By
Aaron W. Baldwin

The Mark of Elyon
The Warrior of Elyon

The Choice for Grace

The Honor of Elyon

A novel by

Aaron W. Baldwin

Divine River Publishing

ISBN:0692755357
ISBN-13: 978-0692755358

DEDICATION

This book is dedicated to the fans.

ACKNOWLEDGMENTS

I would like to thank Keri and Brenda for helping me with their insights after reading really rough drafts. I would like to thank Kit for not giving up on this project. As always I would like to thank my wife, Regina for listening to every idea, some good and some bad, even when she did not want to. Mostly I would like to thank God for the inspiration for the ideas and words to share as well as putting these amazing people in my life to help me.

chapter 1

A mournful, hollow wail pierced the crisp morning air waking the people of the nearby village. Stories circulated among the peasants about how the ghost of the old king haunted the halls of the castle. Many people avoided the forest just north of the castle for fear of the creatures that lived in those woods. Creatures they only saw in their nightmares.

Very few people ventured into the forest after dark. None that returned to share their story anyway. Dragons had been spotted in recent days in the air over the lake hidden by the trees. Villagers believed banshees lived in the woods ready to to drag the souls of wanderers to the underworld.

The cry of the morning did nothing to dispel the rumors, stories and superstitions of the villagers. At worst the awful howl provided further evidence of beliefs the villagers held. At best the sound woke the children who now joined the call with their own cries of fear.

The cry filled the castle and triggered a general call to arms among the guards. The warriors who lived within Bekah's stone walls scrambled to answer the alarm. The cry carried outside the castle walls to the forest and nearby village. Many of the soldiers also believed that the castle was haunted.

Many of the defenders of the castle were raised in the nearby villages. They shared the belief that the forest just north of the castle housed the creatures of their nightmares. Still they rushed toward the howl that shattered the morning peace. The shrieking sounded again and filled the air for several minutes. Then it ceased mysteriously before it suddenly erupted once more.

Several castle guards followed their commander up the spiral staircase. The cry grew louder with each step. The only sound they made came from the clattering of their weapons and armor as they ran. Their commander stopped outside of the bed chamber of the king's highest ranked advisor. The source of the howl seemed to come from behind the door. With his sword drawn, Atherton opened the door slowly and cautiously.

"Kenneth, is everything alright?" the former guardian asked. His friend did not answer. As Atherton stepped inside the room he saw why.

Kenneth Tudyck stood over his weeping wife. She sat on the floor and rocked back and forth. Her arms cradled a small bundle. Atherton dismissed the guards with him, giving the order that all should return to their normal posts and sheathed his own sword. The soldiers quickly complied and left the commander to speak to the king's advisor.

Atherton had never truly felt this way before. He had been among humans for centuries so he recognized the feeling but experienced grief now for the first time. As one of Elyon's nearly immortal guardians he had not known real pain or sadness. Any being that lived in Elyon's presence in paradise remained in constant joy. He missed paradise but momentarily rejoiced that the child now experienced the joy of Elyon. The child would never know the pain of this world.

Since Elyon exiled him for disobedience, Atherton now felt what humans felt. He grew tired and hungry. He now needed food and sleep in order to function. He shared in their joy when the baby was brought home safely from the demon Charax's attempt at sacrificing the child. He now felt the pain in the hearts of the little one's parents as he watched the still bundle tightly clutched in his mother's arms. He knew he could not completely know their pain but Atherton hurt because they hurt.

He joined Kenneth and Krysta in the middle of the room. Kenneth looked up at his friend, as Atherton stood head and shoulders over most men. Kenneth did not try to hide his grief or tears. Atherton glanced back to the door.

The king's two newest advisors stood just inside the room. Vanacore stood, as silent as ever, dressed all in black. Roland Melkin leaned against the doorpost, heartless and uncaring. He sucked at his teeth and picked at his fingernails with one of his throwing knives. The bald man's callousness angered Kenneth but his pain pushed away the anger.

Kenneth returned to Krysta and knelt next to his wife. She continued to rock but stopped the wailing. Fresh tears poured down her soft and already tearstained cheeks. Kenneth gently placed a hand on her back. She stopped rocking. She lowered the bundle that she clutched to her chest. Their newborn son lay in her arms, unmoving with a pale gray hue to his face.

"He's dead, Atherton. Sometime in the night..." Kenneth started. He fought to keep his composure but just let his words drop off.

Nothing more needed to be said. Atherton glanced back at the door. Vanacore nudged Roland and with a slight nod of his head, motioned toward the hall. Without a word the pair slipped out of the room. A moment later, King Lyons quietly entered. He crossed halfway across the room. Kenneth stood and met the king.

"My son is dead," Kenneth said as he looked his long time friend squarely in his lightening blue eyes.

The king did not move or say anything for a long moment. "I am sorry for your loss," he said finally as he dropped his eyes to the stone floor.

Then he turned and left without another word. Atherton noted the surprise on Kenneth's face. The king's response left him speechless.

Atherton understood that people mourn in their own ways but expected more from the king. Kenneth had been there for King Ethan as he mourned his father and the loss of Mina, the love of his life.

The king never left Kenneth's side when he mourned his own father after learning the truth of who he was. These two men had grown up together as close to brothers as two men from different families could be. They were each other's next of kin. It was a bond that Atherton did not fully understand but hoped maybe someday he could.

Kenneth did not know what to expect from Ethan but the reaction he received was the furtherest from his mind. He felt his friend could have at least offered a comforting word. Ethan always talked about how Elyon provided him the words he needed to give in any situation.

Words of wisdom or comfort were handed out to the people as they came to the king with their concerns. Now of all occasions Kenneth thought Ethan would have more to say than 'I'm sorry for your loss'. They had always leaned on each other times of crisis. They had experienced many of them throughout the years. This was not like Ethan.

Perhaps he just does not know what to say because he has never lost a child, Kenneth thought.

Quickly he pushed the thought aside as Krysta began to sob loudly once again. He returned to her side as Atherton quietly exited the room. As much as his grief hollowed out his heart and soul, he would have to find a way to stay strong for his wife. Someone once told him that time healed all wounds. Time healed physical wounds for sure. He knew emotional wounds took longer to heal. He questioned if this cut to his soul would ever completely heal. Time would tell. Only Elyon knew for sure.

Elyon, he thought. *Why did you do this?*

Kenneth's tears flowed down his cheeks like water from the river that broke through the dam. He thought about the benevolent god that Elyon was supposed to be. The god Ethan served. The god that Ethan's Uncle Rufus served until his death. The god that Atherton continued to serve after being exiled from this so called good and kind god's service.

I do not see your kindness, Elyon, Kenneth thought. *In fact I see that you have been unfair to Atherton and to me.*

"Why did you take my son?" he whispered. He wanted to run out into the forest and scream his question as loud as he could manage. Instead he broke down into his own violent sobs as he screamed his question over and over in his head.

He felt his anger rise. He wanted to stand up and curse Elyon from the top of the castle's highest tower. He wanted to shout his anger so the whole kingdom would hear about how Elyon was so unfair to them.

Then another word formed inside his thoughts. Peace. It was a soft voice that spoke this time. Definitely not his own. Over and over just the one word. The turbulent storm of anger raging inside his spirit slowly ceased. The peace the voice spoke of replaced the anger. His sobs stopped but the tears still flowed. Krysta too had stopped sobbing. Perhaps she heard the voice too. Kenneth held his wife while she held their son. He allowed the peace to fill him but wondered how long it would last.

chapter 2

Benniah woke to a bone chilling cry from somewhere above him. His cheek lay flat against a cold, stone floor. His mouth was dry and his head pounded like it had been used as a blacksmith's anvil. He slowly pushed himself to his knees. His wrists were chained together. A second chain, three times longer than the first connected the chain between his shackles to an iron loop embedded into the stone floor. The chain that held him to the floor only allowed him enough slack to remain on his knees, seated or lying on the floor.

He pushed himself to his knees and looked around to take in his surroundings. Stone walls matched the floor. There were no windows in the room. The only light he saw shimmered through the small window on the wooden door and the crack along where the door and stone met.

Other than the fact that he still lived, he had no way to determine the time of day. He assumed since his head was still attached the sun had not set again yet.

He pulled on the chains but the iron loop did not move. He expected as much. He thought he had to try anyway. He relaxed and resolved that he was going to die. Until then he determined to solve the riddles that had been placed in front of him. He would try no matter how little time he had left.

First, he closed his eyes and tried to remember his past. He knew if he could remember something, anything, about who he was then he could begin to unlock the riddles he faced. He remembered washing up on the beach on Rathua, meeting Meldorn and being exiled from the island by Gomaere Wakenda. He remembered Amber Maras and the rescue of her parents. He remembered the battle with the Najera rider called Famine and an urgent feeling that he had to speak to the King of Eden. No matter how hard the tried, nothing before the beach came back to him. He opened his eyes.

Benniah considered the previous conversation with King Lyons. Even more questions filled his mind and replaced his failed attempt at calling up the past. How did the king know Gomaere Wakenda? Who was the king's brother? Why did Benniah feel drawn to Eden to speak to the king? Most importantly, why would the king take his memory away with a spell? The more he pondered those questions the more confused and disappointed he became. He released an audible sigh. His shoulders drooped at the prospect of his death.

"Your will be done, Lord Elyon," he said.

He moved from his knees to his seat and crossed his legs in front of him with his knees pointed out to his sides. He took another deep breath and released it. He closed his eyes again and began to do the thing Meldorn had taught him to do when he did not know what else to do. Pray.

He asked Elyon for the answers to his various questions. He asked for deliverance from the sentence the king imposed on him. Mostly he prayed for peace. He asked for peace to his friends and peace to the land of Tilibra. He asked for the peace to meet death if this would indeed be his end.

He found, as he sat there making his requests to Elyon, he began to worship his God. The longer he prayed and worshipped, the greater the peace he asked for filled him. Soon he did not even feel the shackles on his wrists or the chains that bound him. Somehow he felt like he was free no matter where his body was.

The opening of the cell door brought him out of his trance. The bald man called Roland entered, followed by another guard who carried a tray with a wooden bowl and a cup. Benniah looked up and smiled.

"I suppose you are here to cut off my head," he said to the man.

Roland smiled showing off all of his crooked and yellow teeth. With a hawk like nose, icy cold glare and pale skin he looked a lot like the Najera that Benniah destroyed in Tilibra. Although, something in his spirit told him that Roland was more dangerous.

Roland stroked his goatee. "No, it is not that time yet. However, I am looking forward to executing you. Just so you know, I have no intention of starting with your head."

"Thanks for the warning," Benniah said with a smile as he tried to supress the shudder he felt coming on. Roland seemed to take joy in the thought of torturing Benniah. "If you are not here to kill me, why are you here?"

"The king ordered me to give you another chance to change your mind."

"Change my mind about what?" Benniah asked. He knew the answer to the question but hoped he could goad Roland into giving up some information just in case he would be able to escape.

"He wants to give you another chance to worship him and save your insignificant life," Roland replied as he circled the prisoner. Again Benniah felt as if he was being circled by a wolf.

"I will not worship any man," Benniah answered.

He remembered Meldorn saying something about there not being any gain for a man to be given everything in this world and lose his soul by worshipping another god. Despite Roland's attempt to intimidate him, peace still filled Benniah's spirit.

"I hoped you would say that." The man's grin widened. "In fact, I told the king as much. I told him it was just a waste of time. I have come across men like you before. Committed to this god or that cause.

"It doesn't matter what you are committed to. You'll put on a brave face until you are dragged to the executioner's block. Then you will cry like a little child and beg to betray your convictions. By then it will be too late. You will die slowly and painfully."

Benniah did not speak. He squared his shoulders as a show of defiance. He hoped he would not become just another one of those men who lost their dignity and conviction at the last moment.

"Did you know there are hundreds of techniques to use to cut a man so that he feels the pain but does not experience the release of death?" Roland asked.

"No, but it seems like a good skill for someone like you to have."

"Not only do I know them all, I created some of them," Roland ignoring Benniah's quips. His smile now looked more like a wolf's snarl.

"You are not only educated but an innovator too," Benniah said. He forced his own smile to remain on his face.

Peace still filled his spirit but he felt fear as it crept in and threaten to break his peace. Each breath Benniah took came to him quicker than the last. His body fought to betray his thoughts. The bald man stopped right in front of him. His smile and snarl both now gone. Evidently he did not appreciate Benniah's confidence. This time Benniah could not stop the shudder from creeping down his spine.

"Since you are in a sharing mood. Why would the king use a spell to take my memory away?"

The other squatted down so that their eyes locked at the same level. He smiled like a hunter who had cornered his prey. Roland poked Benniah's forehead a couple of times with his boney forefinger.

"You really don't remember who you are?" Roland chuckled and then stood.

"So are you going to tell me?" Benniah asked after a long pause.

Roland took the bread from the tray held by the guard. He tore a piece off and tossed it into his mouth. Slowly he turned to fully face Benniah again.

"I will make you a deal." The predatory grin returned. "I will tell you, *if* you beg for your life."

Benniah sat just as he was when Roland entered. His knees began to ache and the pain shot straight up his back but he did not move, not even to shift the stress on his knees. Still he smiled at the other. "I guess you will keep that secret to my grave."

The bald man's smile disappeared as his face twisted into a scowl. The man's smug attitude quickly changed. Hate burned from his eyes. He took the tray from the guard, snorted and then spit into the wooden bowl. He half smiled again and dropped the tray in front of Benniah. The stew and water splashed over the edges of their containers. Roland kicked the bowl onto the prisoner.

"Enjoy your meal," he said. "It will be your last."

Though angered by the mercenary's actions, Benniah allowed the peace to come out instead. "Thank you. I will," he said as Roland turned to leave. "I'll see you at sundown."

The bald man stopped and looked back over his left shoulder. He swiftly turned with his right hand drawn back. The last thing Benniah saw was Roland's fist come in from his left. A moment later he felt the left side of his head struck. He fell over as blackness took him.

chapter 3

Again Benniah woke with his head on the floor. It pounded even harder than before. He opened his eyes wide but his vision just blurred. Not that there was much for him to see yet. He realized he laid on his stomach with one cheek on the cold floor. His vision slowly cleared. He did not move. Instead he chose to remain where he lay. His body ached and the peace he felt before had not yet returned. He hoped after Roland's blow part of his memory would return. No new memories came to him, only pain.

Now he truly accepted the fact that he would die soon. He determined he would not beg for his life or bow to anyone or anything to save himself. He would die with dignity and honor. He still had no idea how much time remained before the bald man returned to carry out his sentence.

From the other side of the door he heard shuffling like someone approached the cell. The sound changed from a shuffle to a scuffle. The men outside fought with someone or something. Someone crashed against the door with a hard thud. All fell silent again. Benniah strained to hear any indication of what happened on the other side of the door.

The key scraped the inside of the lock as someone slowly inserted and turned it. He barely heard the click of the catch inside the lock as it released, above the sound of his pounding heart. Benniah tried to summon the peace he felt before. It refused to return. The chill of fear took over. He shivered. He expected to see the mercenary's face when the door opened.

Benniah pushed himself to his knees as quickly as his chains and aching body allowed. The door opened to reveal a mercenary but not the one he expected. The man dressed in all black stood before him. As hard as he tried, Benniah could not remember the man's name. Manticore was all that came to mind.

The pain in his head did not allow him to think clearly. *It must be time to die,* he thought.

It took him another moment before he realized the man in black came alone. Roland promised *he* would be Benniah's executioner. Now Benniah became very confused. He wondered if he were just seeing things because of the multiple blows from Roland to his head.

A silver flash came at him and cut through his chains. The other man quickly rushed back out and dragged one of the guards into the cell. He pointed at the man on the ground and then at Benniah.

"Put on his clothes," the man said in a soft muffled whisper and stepped outside the door. Benniah wasted no further time and began to remove the guard's uniform.

It took him a few minutes to put the new outfit on. He fumbled with the garments because of his chains and the pain and stiffness in his lower body. The unconscious man was a little bigger than Benniah. The sleeves on the shirt and legs of the trousers were a touch too long. He hoped no one would look too closely as he put on the helmet.

When the man in black returned he handed Benniah his own sword. The sword had washed up on the beach of Rathua with him. So he assumed it was his.

King Ethan claimed the weapon belonged to him when he locked Benniah in this dungeon. The other motioned for Benniah to follow. The man in black closed and locked the door behind them. Benniah noticed how the other guard sat in front of the door apparently asleep. He knew the man did not sleep. He was unconscious or dead. Benniah hoped the guard would wake up eventually.

"Vanacore," Benniah whispered. His head had cleared some and the other man's name came to him. The man in black looked over at him. "Your name is Vanacore."

The man nodded and raised one finger to his covered mouth to indicate for Benniah to remain quiet. The man waved Benniah forward. Benniah followed close as Vanacore led him through the dungeon. He thought it was odd that he somehow knew which turns the other was about to make going through the maze of halls. Quietly they moved until Vanacore motioned for him to stop where two halls crossed.

The man in black peeked around the corner. Apparently satisfied with what he saw, he stepped out from his cover and motioned for Benniah to stay where he stood. Benniah moved up to the corner. Slowly, he peeked around to see for himself but he missed all of the action. Vanacore already disarmed and knocked out a single guard who blocked their path.

Benniah stepped into the open as Vanacore gently placed the guard in a dark corner. The prisoner and liberator continued their silent journey to escape the castle. Vanacore led Benniah down another dimly lit hall.

Vanacore moved like a shadow across the floor. Even his weapons refused to rattle as he gracefully walked the halls. Benniah struggled to keep the chains still attached to his wrists silent as they made their way to the exit.

Voices, footsteps and the clattering of armor could be heard from up ahead. Vanacore shoved Benniah into a dark corner and pulled a black cloak over their heads. Benniah struggled to control his breathing. His rescuer put a finger to his covered mouth again as warning to keep quiet. The marching soldiers passed without noticing the two in the corner. Roland's course voice could be heard barking orders to the men.

Time was running out. In a matter of minutes the bald man would discover Benniah missing and the alarm would be sounded. They had to get out of the castle and get out quickly. Otherwise, Benniah was certain, two heads would be removed this evening.

Vanacore dropped the cloak and motioned for Benniah to follow. They moved faster now. His liberator surely knew what was at stake for both of them if they were caught. The man in black led him to the kitchen. A cook looked up as they entered but quickly returned his attention to the meat he was preparing. No one else paid any attention to the king's mysterious lieutenant and a single soldier whose uniform did not quite fit.

Servants worked hard cutting vegetables, preparing beef and baking bread for the king's evening meal. The smell of the fresh bread baking in the hearth made Benniah's stomach growl. He had not eaten anything for about a day and a half now. Roland basically wasted Benniah's last meal. There was not time to stop and eat now. They had to get away. By now Roland should have found the guard in his undergarments alone in the cell he once occupied.

Vanacore stopped at the kitchen door that led to the garden. He motioned for Benniah to wait and exited. The final rays of light lit the garden area. Roland would find the guards at any moment now. Benniah wished his rescuer would hurry but silently watched through the open door as Vanacore approached two guards who eyed the waiting horses.

The first guard spoke to Vanacore who answered with several hand gestures. The second guard kept looking at the horses and glanced back toward Benniah in the kitchen. He tried to look like he was supposed to be there but the second guard looked suspicious.

One of the servants bumped into Benniah. "Watch it. What are you doing in here anyway?" she asked. The suspicious guard took a step toward the open door.

Benniah did not witness the other scuffles this mysterious man had been part of on this rescue but was surprised by how quickly the next fight happened.

With one hand he grabbed the second guard by the arm and pulled him back from the door. His opposite foot connected with the side of the head of the first guard and knocked him to the ground. The second guard swung a fist at Vanacore. He missed his only chance to land a punch against the man in black. Benniah's new ally dodged the strike and countered with a quick jab to the nose, followed by a punch to the throat and a front kick to his chest. All three strikes landed within just a matter of seconds. The man fell to the ground holding his throat.

The first guard regained his senses and stood. Vanacore's back faced the guard as he watched to ensure the second man did not rejoin the fight.

"Vanacore!" Benniah yelled in warning.

His rescuer seemed to be jerked backwards but Benniah realized the man jumped. He kicked his feet up and completed a back flip. The top of his right foot smashed into the head of the first guard. Vanacore landed hard on the ground and did not move for several seconds. The kick stunned the guard but he did not fall.

Benniah felt his feet move before he realized he had taken action. He ran from his spot in the kitchen and crashed headfirst into the guard. He heard a gasp as they hit the ground. Benniah smashed his fist on the other man's temple and watched as his eyes as they rolled back into his head. Slowly Benniah stood.

Vanacore handed him the reins to one of the horses. He led Benniah to an iron gate in the wall to the rear of the garden. Alarm bells rang out.

Everyone now knew he no longer occupied his cell. With Vanacore in front they led the horses through the gate because it was not tall enough for them to ride through. After Benniah came out on the other side, Vanacore calmly closed the gate and locked it with a chain.

The two mounted their horses and rode hard northwest to the forest. They rode along the deer paths for a short time until the light of the sun finally died out for the day. They heard no one pursuing them. Vanacore slowed his horse and led at a brisk pace as opposed to a full gallop.

This pace is too dangerous to ride in the dark, Benniah thought but did not speak his concern. The other man apparently knew the trails well enough.

They stopped for a moment where the tree line met a sandy beach. Clouds conspired to hide the moon and stars on this night and made the still, glasslike surface of the lake look black.

Vanacore motioned for Benniah to follow. The man in black did not seem concerned by pursuers now as he led at a leisurely walk. They remained in the trees as they silently rode. Benniah followed for what seemed to be another hour before speaking.

"Where are we going? Why are you helping me?"

Vanacore kept riding and did not respond to the questions. Benniah knew the man could talk. He used his voice back at the castle.

Benniah had no more patience for the games the other man seemed to be playing. Benniah needed answers. Specifically why the mysterious man risked his life to help Benniah escape. Exhaustion had taken over his body as the rush of energy he felt during his escape faded. He had not eaten or drank anything in about two days. Hungry, sore and stiff, he was determined to get answers now.

He stopped his horse. "I appreciate your effort in helping me escape but I think this is where we part ways," Benniah said.

Vanacore stopped. He looked out onto the beach and urged his horse forward out onto the sand with a heel to the animal's flanks.

"You deserve answers. Follow me and you will have them," he replied in his muffled voice.

Benniah watched as another pair of men appeared afar off on the beach. In the dark Benniah could not judge how far away they were from the other men. Vanacore rode forward like he expected to meet the men here by the lake. Benniah doubted he would get anymore answers than he already had. Not now at least.

Reluctantly, he followed. He stopped next to his rescuer. The other men would join them in a matter of moments. Benniah took advantage of the time and attempted to get his questions answered again.

"Why don't we start with why you are doing this?"

"Soon," Vanacore answered. He removed a wineskin off of his saddle, pulled the mask up to expose a pair of soft pink lips surrounded by pale white skin. Benniah thought it unusual for a man but dismissed the thought. Vanacore took a small sip and handed the wineskin to Benniah who eagerly accepted it. He drank heavily. The warm liquid tasted like ordinary water instead of wine. Some fluid leaked from the corners of his mouth but he did not care if it ran down his chin. His mouth and throat felt like a desert.

"Do not fight it," Vanacore said as Benniah took a second, long drink.

Benniah's vision began to blur. He quickly realized the water had been poisoned. He let the wineskin fall to the ground and spill out on the sand. The last he remembered was being gently lowered to the ground from his horse before his world turned black.

chapter 4

King Lyons sat at his desk in his private study. Atherton, Ulysses and several officers stood in a semicircle in front of the desk. With a centaur in the room it seemed like the king stuffed the entire army in the study. Roland Melkin leaned against the bookshelves behind the king.

Kenneth stood on the opposite side of the room from the bald man. His arms folded across his chest as he gazed off into space. To the casual observer, he looked like he simply stared at the backs of his friends. The truth was his mind was not on the topic of discussion at all. He still thought about the death of his son. He cared nothing about a prisoner escape.

I should be with Krysta right now, he thought. *No at some strategy meeting.*

"What are your excuses again?" Ethan asked the officers.

"Majesty, we were able to track the fugitives to the forest but it is too dark in the forest at night to track them further," replied the highest ranked officer.

"A troll could have tracked them to the forest. That is the most logical place for them to go," the king said. He made no effort to hide the anger and disgust in his tone.

"Majesty, if I may," Ulysses said. The centaur was Eden's high general and captain of the king's guards. "The forest can be a dark place during the day but at night, even with torches, it would be nearly impossible to search for them safely."

"I'm not worried about their safety. I want them returned, dead or alive and I want them now," the king answered as he stood and slammed one fist on the desk.

"I was referring to the safety of *my* men," the centaur said. His muscles tensed and his coppery horse end shifted.

Ethan upset Ulysses but Kenneth knew the centaur would not push the matter much further. If the king commanded, Kenneth knew Ulysses would go out and search until he found the fugitives. Atherton would do the same. Ordinarily, so would Kenneth but he was in no mood to follow the whim of his friend tonight.

"Why do you want them caught so badly? What did this Benniah do to deserve to be imprisoned in the first place, Ethan?" Kenneth asked. He also made no effort to hide the disgust in his voice. His friend hardly ever imprisoned anyone and had never done so without telling him who the prisoner was and why he was being held.

The king pointed at the officers and commanded them to leave. Melkin escorted them to the door and closed it behind them. On his return to the king's side, Roland stopped next to Kenneth. The bald man stared at the king's friend with a twisted grin on his face.

Kenneth turned to face the man. He lowered his arms and silently hoped Roland would start something, anything. With all of the emotions boiling inside, Kenneth thought he could win a fight with an ogre. He would take great satisfaction in beating the bald man senseless. A fight may even be a good way to relieve some of the stress and anger that currently surged through his mind, soul and body.

Roland seemed to be of the same mind. His grin widened and he took a slightly more aggressive posture. Kenneth tensed and flexed his fingers and transformed his open hands to clenched fists. Kenneth heard Ulysses' hooves clatter against the stone floor as he shifted around, most likely to intervene.

"Kenneth," the king shouted and drew attention from the standoff back to him. "You need to stop addressing me in such an informal manner, especially in front of those who are ranked under you."

Kenneth tilted his head slightly at the statement. Ethan had been king for more than five years and never before mentioned the way any of his close friends addressed him.

"Why is that even important? Right now, I need you to answer my other questions."

"It is important because I am the king and as king I deserve a certain amount of respect. When you address me so informally, you do not show me the proper respect. Allowing such lack of respect among the army makes me look weak among the ranks. Eden cannot afford a weak king."

"That is what this is about? Respect? Looking weak?" Kenneth asked as he approached the desk. "That's why you want these men so badly? Because a man you barely knew helped another man escape your dungeon."

"How dare you question my motives," the king replied. He pointed his finger at Kenneth. "The only thing you need to know is I want them found. It makes no difference why."

Kenneth threw his hands in the air and turned his back to his friend. "This is ridiculous."

"Do *not* turn your back on me," the king commanded. Kenneth turned to face him again. "I understand you are in mourning but this is not how you act in the presence of your king."

"Is there anything else I can do for you, *Majesty*?" Kenneth asked. Each word he spoke in an almost mocking tone. Especially the final word.

"You are dismissed. I suggest you return to your wife before I put *you* in the dungeon."

Livid, Kenneth held all further words that came to mind. It was clear that he was not going to change his friend's mind. He thought it best just to end the argument before he said something he would regret.

This was not their first argument. They had grown up together as brothers and had argued many times. One argument when they were children was resolved when Ethan threw a small shield at him. The cut left a scar on the bridge of his nose. But in all of their previous arguments, Ethan had never spoken so demeaning to him.

"As you wish, Majesty," Kenneth said. He crossed one foot in front of the other, bent at the waist and waved his other arm out in a wide sweeping motion, in a formal bow. When he stood upright again, he turned to the door and exited. He slammed the door behind him to emphasize his point. A moment later he heard his name.

He turned to see the centaur had followed him. More muscles than Kenneth thought possible lined the human torso of his centaur friend. A life in the sun with no shirt left Ulysses with perfectly tanned skin. The strong square jaw and well defined cheekbones made his face appear to have sculpted by the greatest artist in the land. Long dark, brown hair topped his head and grew into a mane that lined the center of his back.

Ulysses was loyal to Ethan and had become a good friend to both he and Ethan but Kenneth did not want to hear any speeches right now. Atherton's tall, blonde figure stopped beside Ulysses.

"What?" Kenneth asked. He shook his head and pointed one finger at the door behind them. "There's nothing you can say to me to justify how he spoke to me."

"We are not going to try to justify anything," Atherton replied. Kenneth had to look up to look the former guardian in his dark grey eyes. Atherton stood head and shoulders over most men.

"He should not speak to me like that. I have been his friend all of his life. There is something wrong with him. He would not keep secrets from me. He would never talk to anyone like that especially his closest friends."

"I admit his behavior has been unusual since his return," the centaur stated.

"Unusual? That is not the word for it. He is not himself and I don't know who he is," Kenneth said. He paced a few steps and turned around as he continued.

"He has never spoken to me like that. Ever. He has never turned down a friend but when Kiat asked for help to free his people, Ethan refused. Not that long ago Ethan tried to convince me that the Tulchin elves in Qantas were our allies but now he turned his back on them."

Kenneth paused and looked to the floor to hide the tears that filled his eyes. He could not be sure if it was because of the pain he felt due to the death of the baby or because he felt like his friend betrayed him. "He did not even blink when I told him my son died."

The other two stood silent for a moment. None of them moved. Kenneth did not know what to expect from them next.

Ulysses spoke first. "You two will have to keep an eye on him. I am going to search for the fugitives alone."

"Why not just let Melkin handle it?" Kenneth asked.

"I think they have some of the answers we are looking for and I do not believe Roland will exercise the restraint to bring them back alive."

"May Elyon bless your path," Atherton said.

"May He bless both of yours as well," the centaur replied. They shook hands and Kenneth watched his friend leave before he returned to his grieving wife.

Roland waited for the centaur and the guardian to exit the study. He closed the door behind them. He had hoped Kenneth would have thrown a punch so he could go ahead and kill the man now. He had the skills to kill any man. He had killed lots of men. Some for profit. Some just because he felt the urge to kill. If he had to defend himself, he would have had a justifiable reason to kill Tudyck.

Self-defense is just not as much fun as hunting a man down, he thought.

"Perhaps you overreacted to the informal way he spoke to you. After all, he is used to calling his friend by his given name and not any title," Roland said.

"Maybe," the king replied. He paused a moment to consider the mercenary's words. "To keep up appearances, I will apologize to him later when he has calmed down. We have come too close to fail now because he becomes suspicious."

"He is already suspicious. He has been suspicious since we returned. I thought we should have killed him then. Would you like me to take care of him now?"

"No. I still need him."

"What are your orders regarding Vanacore?" Roland asked as he slowly walked back to the desk.

"Find him. Find them both. Kill them both. Send the centaur away in the morning. He could become a problem."

"I could kill him too."

"No. Just send him away."

The king sat down in the chair and rubbed his temples. He did not need this right now. "I wanted to have the medallion before I made my display but we will move that up."

"How soon?"

"As soon as possible and then everyone will worship me as more than a king."

chapter 5

Blurry, white light filled his eyes when Benniah opened them again. After a few moments he saw only white light and realized a sheet had been draped over his head. He drew in a deep breath and sat up. The sudden movement caused his world to spin. He closed his eyes again and took a couple of deep breathes to fight the dizziness that came over him. Once his head no longer spun, Benniah removed the sheet and opened his eyes.

Sunlight filled the room through an open window. He sat on a comfortable bed in a white room. A small table near the door was the only other piece of furniture in the room. A multicolored blanket lay at the foot of the bed. He tried to remember the events of the night before.

He recalled sitting on his horse and drinking the water offered by Vanacore. Again he searched his memory for something further back than washing up on Rathua. Again he found nothing more.

He swung his legs over the side of the bed. His bare feet touched the stone floor and surprisingly the floor did not feel cold. He looked down at the blue robes he wore and wondered how he got into them. He did not remember changing his clothes. He stood, stretched and dismissed the thought. A sharp pain shot through his back as he moved.

"That does not feel like I am in paradise," he said.

An old man shuffled into the room. He carried a tray with bread, fruit and a wood cup and porcelain pitcher on it. He placed the tray on the small table and shuffled to Benniah.

"Glad to see you are back in the land of the living," he said. Wrinkles etched his tanned face but his green eyes remained sharp. A friendly smile crossed his face yet Benniah felt as if the man had something to hide. Perhaps he felt that way because most of the people he met recently had kept secrets of some kind from him.

"I was dead?" Benniah asked.

"No, I'm sorry. I just meant you had been sleeping hard since the master brought you here," the man replied.

"How long did I sleep?" Benniah asked. He was sure it had to have only been a few hours.

The man placed a hand on his clean shaven chin and tilted his head to the right as he thought. "It has been two days."

"Really? That long." Benniah was angered at this revelation. Vanacore had cost him two days. If they ever met again he would make sure the mysterious man would be properly thanked and then feel his wrath.

"Eat, my lord. I will inform my master that your are awake." With that the servant slowly made his exit.

Benniah realized he had not eaten for over three days. He was a little wary of the offer of food after his experience with Vanacore but his need for sustenance trumped his caution. He tore off a piece of bread and chewed it. He followed it with several more chunks of the soft, warm bread and poured water into the cup.

His throat felt like a dry, dusty road again. He gulped down the water and followed it with another cup. He attacked the fruit next, plucking off a few grapes and tossing them into his mouth one at a time. The sweet juice wet his tongue as the skin burst with each bite.

He passed up the fruit he did not recognize but alternated eating slices of pears, apples and bananas. He stopped for more water and tore off more bread. Even though the meal was a simple he felt like he feasted. When he had his fill he sat on the floor with his back against the bed and sipped water.

He pondered the last few days and tried to answer the various questions in his head but only ended up asking more questions. One clue eluded him. He just did not know where to find it.

He spilled his cup of water as he jumped to his feet when Vanacore entered. *"YOU!"*

Vanacore raised one hand in an attempt to calm Benniah. The black clad warrior knelt and presented Benniah with the sword Meldorn had given to him. Vanacore lowered his head in submission and as a sign of obvious respect. The other man's gesture confused him.

"I have questions," Benniah said after a moment of trying to piece together what was happening. His anger momentary bottled up by this new development.

"You shall have answers," Vanacore said in a soft but muffled voice. "Please take your sword."

Benniah paused a moment and eyed the man dressed in black suspiciously. He knew that his captor was clever and a formidable fighter. He hoped this was not another trap. *If Vanacore wanted to kill you, you would be dead.*

Slowly he reached out and picked up the weapon by the hilt. The double edged sword felt good in his hand. It almost seemed as if the blade had been created just for him. He accepted the weapon but held it at his side. He remained on guard, determined not to fall for any more tricks like he had done two nights ago.

Vanacore lifted his head and slowly pulled the black cloth from off of his face. Benniah sat down on the bed. He did not know how many more new unanswered questions he could take. His head began to spin again as Vanacore revealed his face for the first time. He watched as the mask dropped to the floor. A pale skinned face with brown eyes and soft pink lips stared back at him.

"My name is Mina Derrick," The brown haired woman said.

Benniah stared at the young woman kneeling in front of him for what seemed to be an eternity. Her chestnut hair stopped at the bottom of her ears. He felt he had seen her face before. No matter how hard he tried though, he did not remember from when or where he may have seen her. This was just another mystery he did not need.

"Mina?"

"Yes, my name is Mina," she said rising to her feet.

"I need some answers."

"I will give you all the answers I have," she replied as she walked to him. She sat on the edge of the bed next to him.

"Why did you poison me?" he asked.

"I did not poison you. I gave you a simple sleeping potion so that I could bring you to my secret hideaway. You just drank more of it than I expected."

"Why did you not just blindfold me?"

She blushed and shrugged her shoulders. "I did not really think about that until you had been asleep for a day. " She smiled sheepishly. He found himself liking her smile. "We have more important things to talk about."

"Things like why King Lyons wanted to imprison and execute me?"

"That would be a long story."

"Just start from the beginning."

She paused for a moment. He sensed there was more to her hesitation than simply gathering her thoughts. Then she began. "This is going to sound like a bad fairy tale but I swear to you every word I am about to tell you is true."

He looked at her suspiciously. Something in his spirit warned him to remain vigilant and at the same time he felt he may be able to trust her. He decided to hear her out since this was the closest he had come to getting any answers. "Just tell me and I will decide if I believe you or not."

She took a deep breath and exhaled. "The king is not the king."

His turn to take a deep breath. This *was* going to be hard to believe. "How can the king not be the king?"

"He is not the king because *you* are the king." She paused as this news crept through his mind and into his spirit.

"Wait. What?" he asked.

"You are King Ethan Lyons. You are the King of Eden."

Benniah stood and walked to the other side of the room. He was not sure if he believed her. He raised the sword. "What game are you playing? If I am king who is that man who put me in the dungeon?"

Mina stood and joined him. She gently pushed the sword away. "I am not playing any games with you. I am telling you the truth. You are the king. I swear. Please, sit down and let me finish."

Benniah sighed. He went through the news in his head. The king's response to him made sense if what she said was true. He decided to remain calm and listen. If she was telling the truth he could get some of the answers he needed. He walked to the table and laid the sword down and then returned to sit on the edge of the bed.

"The man you saw is a sorcerer."

"Tell me who you are."

The corners of her mouth pulled up into a slight smile and her cheeks turned red. "That too is a long story."

"Then start at the beginning of that story too," he said.

"Very well," she replied. She sighed this time. "I guess it has been just over five years since we last saw each other. At that time you had asked me to marry you."

"We were to be married?" Benniah stood. Now things really began to sound strange. He paced the floor, unsure if he wanted her to continue. He leaned more toward the idea, that she was making the story up.

"Please sit down," Mina said as she patted the bed next to her. Benniah hesitated a moment longer then returned to his seat. "We were engaged and in love but—,"

He waited for her to finish the statement but when she did not he prompted her for more information. "But what?"

She licked her lips nervously. "I betrayed you."

Mina continued the story without stopping for a while. She told him about his father's death at the hands of a man called Xestes Krollnoss. She explained that her father was once close friends with his father. She told him how her father tried to kill him in order to take the throne and how Krollnoss had ultimately been hired by her father to wipe out the Lyons line. She began to cry as she told Benniah about how she sided with her father and tried to kill him too.

He pulled her close to him and allowed her to cry on his shoulder for several minutes. Between her sobs, she apologized for her betrayal many times. He still had not decided if he believed her story but could not bear to see her cry. Nothing she said to that point caused any memory to return.

Mina stopped her tears and lingered on his shoulder, silently for a moment. "I hope someday you will forgive me," she finally said.

He did not respond. He assumed if his memory returned and all she said was true he would be able to forgive her. She raised her head and smiled weakly.

She sighed again as she sat up straight and wiped her eyes with the palms of her hands. When she had composed herself again she spoke.

"After the battle and my father's death, I swore revenge. I wandered for a few months and found myself in a kingdom north of Tilibra. I met a nobleman who took me in."

She paused a moment, stood and paced the room. Her nervous energy made him feel like he should pace the floor with her. Benniah felt as if she was trying to avoid telling him something. At this point almost nothing she could say would have surprised him. "Go on," he urged.

She stopped pacing. "I thought I had fallen in love with him. Now, I'm not so sure." She stopped and wiped sweat from her forehead. "That is when Alaric invaded. He conquered that kingdom and killed all of the nobles."

"Including the man that you thought you were in love with," Benniah interjected.

She nodded. "Yes, him too."

"Why were you helping him then?"

"I vowed to avenge my love's death. I created the Vanacore persona and eventually won Alaric's trust. I became one of his most trusted—,"

"Advisors?"

"Assassins. Another fact of my life I am ashamed of but that is something I have to work out with Elyon."

"Fair enough." He paused before asking his next question. "Who is Alaric?"

"He is the sorcerer who is disguised as you. An evil sorcerer at that. He wants to conquer every kingdom of the world. He plans on using your identity to unveil the next step of his scheme."

"Which is what?"

"I'm not sure. I heard a lot of talk about Najera but I suspect there is more to it than that."

"The Najera?"

"Yes, they are four ancient riders who—,"

"I know who they are," he interrupted. "There are now three of them."

Mina smiled. "I knew when he mixed that potion that you were more important to the plan than he let on."

"What do you mean?"

"I mean, you can stop him. You just have to remember who you are. That's why he took your memory. That is why he has tried to kill you."

Benniah stood and paced to the other side of the room. "Remembering who I am is easier said than done. I've tried to remember for a while now. The last thing that I remember is waking up on the beach on Rathua."

"You must remember. Not only are you the King of Eden but you are also a Warrior of Elyon. You are the only one who can stop him," she replied. She crossed to him and when she stopped, she placed her hands on his chest.

Benniah took her hands and gently pushed her away. "You don't understand. I just can't remember." He turned his back on her.

"Then Alaric has already won."

She spoke like hope had just been outlawed. When he turned to face her again, she trudged back to the bed with her head down. She sat on the bed quietly, eyes to the floor and hands in her lap. She looked like a scolded dog. He stroked his chin feeling the stubble that grew.

"Tell me more. I understand now why he wanted me executed and I heard him say something to the bald guy about how he thought the ship I was on had been scuttled."

Mina nodded. "Alaric hired a band of pirates to kidnap you as you walked on the beach. Roland was on board the ship and when you had been secured in their brig, you were given the potion. Then Roland was supposed to sink the ship. You and all of the pirates were supposed to drown. The goal was to kill everyone so there would be no witnesses."

"Why bother with removing my memory if I was supposed to die when the ship sank?"

Mina shrugged. "I'm not sure. Alaric really didn't explain to me how the spell worked. He only said the potion would cause you to not remember who you were and as long as you did not know who you were, everyone would see your face when they looked at him."

"Why does he need to look like me?"

Mina shrugged again. "I don't know. He did not say. However, Eden is one of the most powerful kingdoms in the world."

Benniah wanted to believe her. He knew he had to be cautious. He had fallen for the damsel in distress once already with Amber Maras. That was how he became entangled in this mess in the first place. He had to be careful. He placed his hands on top of hers. The softness of her hands sent a familiar wave of excitement through his body. He almost drew them back but he liked the sensation. Perhaps Mina did speak the truth.

"I defeated one of the Najera already, without knowing who I am. I have friends who currently have in their possession the legendary weapons that are supposed to defeat them. If we can stop the Najera, then we can stop Alaric."

Her eyes lit up at once. He was not entirely sure he believed what he had just said. Ever since the fight he had wondered how he defeated the rider called Famine. He should have been killed during the heat wave the creature sent at him. He decided not to worry about how he survived right now and take everything one step at a time. Next he had to make his way back to Prador's estate and regroup with Meldorn and Gerard.

"Alaric and Roland will not stop until they find us," Mina said.

"Then we need to get moving."

They stood as one. "You need to rest. I will make the necessary arrangements for supplies," she said as she started to race from the room.

"Mina, I have one more question."

"Anything."

"Alaric said his brother also tried to kill me. Is his brother Trian Maras?"

Benniah needed to make the connection of how Alaric knew Trian and Wakenda Goemare. If they were brothers then several gaps in this ongoing puzzle would be filled for him. It would be a good plan. Trian usurped the throne of Tilibra. The sorcerer took the place of King Lyons. With Eden, Tilibra and the other kingdom he had already conquered, Alaric would have control of three of the most powerful kingdoms in the world without drawing too much attention to himself. He did not even need a large army to start.

"No."

"No?"

"No. Trian and Alaric are not brothers." She wrinkled her brow and tilted her head as she asked, "I didn't already tell you who his brother was?"

"No, you didn't."

Mina bit her bottom lip. She acted as if she did not want to give him the answer. "Alaric's full name is Alaric Krollnoss. He is the brother of Xestes, the man that killed your father."

Benniah stood there silent, not knowing how to respond. If she had lied to him and made the entire story up then she believed those lies as the truth. If the story were true, why did he not remember? Surely something would have sparked a memory.

"Ethan." He did like the way she said his name. He locked his eyes to hers not because he suddenly believed her but because he just realized how beautiful she really was. "There is one more thing."

He stared a moment longer before speaking. "What is that?"

She hesitated again. He waited impatiently. They could not afford to waste anymore time. They needed to ride. He needed to speak to Meldorn. Perhaps his mentor would be able to help with his memory now that he knew magic was involved.

Mina threw her arms around his neck. She kissed him on his mouth. He accepted the gesture and even kissed her back. He liked her soft lips on his.

A number of feelings stirred in his spirit. Her kiss even felt familiar. When she pulled away he looked into her eyes. He thought something should come back to him but nothing did. Mina must have realized she had either made a mistake or his memory had not returned. The sparkle in her eyes dimmed slightly.

"I'm sorry. I'll get our supplies readied," she said trying to rush by him.

He grabbed her arm and pulled lightly to stop her. "No, it was nice. I still don't remember but I liked it. I hope I do remember. If not I hope this ends soon so we can make new memories."

Her smile returned before she turned and exited the room. He started to believe that they had once been in love but remained cautious. Too many people had already lied to him about who they really were. He could not afford to be wrong again.

chapter 6

Alaric Krollnoss had spent the last two days fuming and allowing his hate to build. He hated Ethan Lyons for escaping. He hated Vanacore for helping him escape. He hated Kenneth for his temper tantrum. He hated Ulysses for disappearing and was getting close to hating Roland for not finding any of them.

Soon the charade would be over and he would kill all of them. Pretending to be King Lyons had become bothersome to him. He despised the man's wholesome image and reputation for being an honorable man. Normally Alaric would have executed the guards who allowed Lyons and Vanacore to escape.

However, King Lyons would be the first to forgive and forget such an egregious error. In order to stay in character he had to forgive these failures too but he would not forget. Soon he would be reassigning these men to the worst possible posts.

Right now he searched for Tudyck. He detested the idea of looking for anyone himself. That was a job for servants and mercenaries. He had told the servants to look for Kenneth but none had found him, at least that is what they claimed. Now Alaric had to search on his own. He approached the door to the Tudyck's chambers. He hoped Kenneth was there and simply ignored his summons.

He did not want to face the man's wife. She would likely still be crying over the death of her son. He smiled to himself. *If she only knew*, he thought. He did not want to face her, not because he felt any guilt for his actions but because a sobbing woman always made him feel uncomfortable. He detested being uncomfortable for any reason more than having to conduct a search for someone himself.

He stopped at the door and knocked. He heard nothing on the inside of the room. He knocked again. Soft footsteps sounded on the stone floor from the other side of the door after the second knock. The door opened and the woman stood in front of him. Silently Alraic cursed.

Red lines seemed to grow from the green in her eyes from tears and lack of sleep. Her bright red hair looked as if she had not run a brush through it since they buried the child two days ago. Her normally pale cheeks were now red and covered with streaks from the paths of the constant tears that poured from her eyes. She still wore her bed clothes from the night before under her open robe. One hand made a feeble attempt to keep the robe closed. In the other hand she held a cloth, no doubt to wipe her eyes and nose.

"Majesty," she said with a bow of her head as she pulled her robe closed tighter. "I'm sorry for my appearance. What can I do for you?"

Alaric's comfort level quickly began to decline but at least she called him by his formal title. Tudyck must have told her about the meeting from the other night. "I am sorry for disturbing you, Krysta. I am looking for Kenneth. Is he here?"

"No, I'm sorry, Eth—, majesty. He went for a ride. I expect that he will be back anytime. I can send him to you when he returns."

"No. I'll go to the stables and leave a message with the servants there." He gave her a weak smile that she returned with the same effort.

Stiffly he turned and made his exit. He heard her close the door behind her as she returned to the sanctuary of the bed chamber. No doubt to continue to cry over the child for another two days.

Alaric had not been to the stables since he showed up at the castle as King Lyons. It took him a while but he found them without asking for directions which would surely have aroused someone else's suspicions.

Tudyck's suspicion was already more than he needed. Alerting another that the king may not be the real king could cause his plan to fail. Better for him to wander aimlessly around the castle than ask a servant for directions. A few minutes later he stood in front of one of the stalls.

He crinkled his nose at the smell of horses, hay and other things he did not even want to think about. He had never been the nature loving, outdoors type of person. That was Xestes. He was the one who rode horses, hunted and generally used his brawn to survive.

For all the good it did him.

Alaric had always relied on his mind, charm and of course magic to get what he wanted. It had served him well in his nearly fifty years of life.

He spotted Kenneth at the last stall brushing his horse. Alaric walked through the barn with swagger and authority. He wanted to be here for as little time as possible. He hoped that Kenneth would not give him trouble and accept his apology.

"Majesty," Kenneth said. He stopped brushing the animal long enough to bow his head. His cold tone told the sorcerer that Tudyck still held hard feelings about their conversation the other night.

"Kenneth, I am sorry for the way I acted in the meeting," Alaric said. The words soured in his mouth. He hated apologizing almost as much as he hated searching for people. It showed weakness. Besides he was king. Tudyck should be groveling at his feet right now but because of Lyons' integrity and honor it would be out of place if he did not apologize.

"Apology accepted, majesty. Is there anything else I can do for you?" Kenneth asked. He voice remained even and emotionless. He responded like a servant who no longer wished to serve his master.

"I overreacted the other night," Alaric said. He paused for effect. He wanted Kenneth to think that Ethan was putting thought into his words instead of Alaric giving a well rehearsed speech. "I was angry. More angry at Vanacore's betrayal than you or anything else."

"I have not trusted him or Roland since the day you returned with them," Kenneth said.

He stopped brushing the horse and faced his king. Alaric noted the look of disgust on the other's face and held his tongue to avoid escalating this situation further.

"I know. You have made your suspicions perfectly clear many times. I guess you deserve to say that you were right. At least about Vanacore."

"That's not what I want, Ethan."

Alaric's anger began to surface again at the mention of that name instead of a title but he managed to let it go. He had to win Kenneth back if his plans were going to occur within the next few days as he wanted. Starting an argument about titles would not help his cause. "Then what do you want?"

"I want you to tell me what is going on. Why are Vanacore and the prisoner so important? Why are you so hung up on titles all of a sudden? What is going on with you?" Kenneth asked.

The sorcerer had no intention of answering any of his questions honestly. The answers would give away his secret and he was not ready to tell the world who he really was yet. "I don't know what you mean."

"I mean refusing to help allies. You sent Kiat away to rescue his people without any aid. You were the one who tried to convince me of the nobility of his efforts at peace. You could have sent me and a legion of soldiers to help him. Instead, when he needs you the most you send him away with no help whatsoever. Not even an escort out of Eden."

"I had other matters to attend to." Alaric struggled to keep his anger at bay. He never allowed anyone to question him in the past. Silently he cursed the name of Ethan Lyons and hoped Lyons' character did not cost him everything. Alaric decided that Tudyck would need to be neutralized sooner than he thought.

After the revealing, if he is not with me then I will let Roland do what he does best.

"More important than saving an enslaved people?"

The sorcerer took authority over the conversation. "You are not king. You do not know the decisions I have to make. Some things have to be sacrificed for the good of Eden. Until you become king you have no right to question my decisions."

Kenneth threw down the brush. Alaric jumped back to avoid the splash of water that leapt from the bucket the brush landed in but was unsuccessful at avoiding it.

"Listen to yourself. We have known each other for over thirty years. Since we were children. I grew up with you in this very castle watching your father rule. For the last five years I have watched you rule. I think I know a little about what decisions you have to make." Kenneth's hands flew all around as he spoke.

Kenneth pushed past Alaric trying to storm away. Shocked at how the other just spoke to him, the sorcerer could not say a word. Quickly he regained his composure and turned before Kenneth could exit the barn.

"I have an assignment for you."

Tudyck stopped but did not turn around. "Really? What would that be?" This time his emotionless tone bordered on disrespect.

Alaric walked to face Kenneth. He stared him in the eyes as he explained his instructions. It surprised him that it was not hate he saw in the other's eyes but more like sadness, like he had been disappointed about something.

Still the sorcerer was glad to be getting to the reason for the visit. He thought he began to reek of the smell of horses and wanted to leave. He explained to Tudyck how he wanted him to complete all of the arrangements for his big announcement. He explained how and where the dais was to be built and ordered that riders be sent with news for all to gather in the fields between Bekah and Nain.

"What is this all about?" Kenneth asked.

"Good things are going to begin to happen to this kingdom and through Eden good things will flow throughout the world."

"What kind of good things?" Kenneth's curiosity had been piqued.

Alaric took this as a sign he could still win Kenneth back despite the uncharacteristic behavior. *Tudyck would make an excellent ally if he does not need to be eliminated.*

"Miracles, Kenneth. Many great and wonderful miracles. Elyon has told me that you and Krysta are going to receive the greatest miracle," the sorcerer replied with a smile.

Kenneth did not return the smile. He bowed dutifully. "It will be as you have commanded."

"Good. I'm counting on you, Kenneth," Alaric said widening his grin. He walked out of the barn with even more swagger, leaving Tudyck standing alone. He decided to go straight to a bath and to have the clothes he wore burned.

chapter 7

Only five men volunteered to ride with Benniah and Mina. Benniah would have liked to have had more but these five were all that volunteered. He did not look like the King of Eden. He did not even look like a king. He had no army behind him. He could not blame any man for not volunteering. He was not even sure if he would have volunteered if he were given their choice. The people he sought to challenge were very dangerous. If he did not believe Mina's story why should anyone else.

As he rode, he thought about her tale. Some of it made sense. Some of it agreed with things Meldorn had told him. Specifically the part about him being a Warrior of Elyon. Still she had been working with a man who ordered his execution just a few days ago. He decided he would have to remain vigilant until he remembered. After all, in her own words she had tried to kill him before, *if* he believed her story.

Benniah led Mina and her men north and west from their village. He hoped Gerard had made it back to Jonathan

Prador's estate with the weapons and the medallion. If not he had no idea on how to defeat Alaric or the Najera. As he rode he thought about the report that he had to take to the others. No one would have suspected King Lyons as being aligned with Maras and Wakenda but somehow he was. Or this impostor was, again, *if* he believed Mina's story.

He allowed his mind to wander as he rode. He grew weary just thinking about the questions that have plagued him. He no longer wished to think about the questions, the missing answers and the answers Mina had provided. There just seemed to be too many pieces of the puzzle still missing. He thought some of Mina's story should have made him remember something but nothing came back to him. He thought her kiss definitely should have made him remember, if they were who she said they were.

He thought about the kiss and glanced to his right where Mina rode next to him. Her story may have been a lie but the kiss they shared was real.

He felt the connection and passion between them. Deep down in a small corner of his spirit he wanted to believe her. He felt like he needed to believe her tale. His heart desperately wanted to believe because that would mean he could reclaim at least a portion of his past and he could have a future with her. He hoped he could have a future with her even if he never remembered another detail of his past. They had to defeat their enemies first.

She caught him as he stared at her and flashed a shy smile. He felt his face turn red. He returned the sheepish grin and snapped his attention back to the horizon in front of him.

"Anything coming back to you?" she asked.

"What?" He knew what she had asked but wanted to seem like he had not been paying attention to her. He wanted to try to not make it so awkward. They both knew he had failed miserably but she played along and asked him again.

"Is any of your memory returning? I mean, after our—," Mina hesitated.

"Discussion?" Benniah guessed that the men who followed knew nothing of their kiss or supposed previous relationship. He decided they would keep it between themselves. Benniah shook his head.

"No, nothing yet." Her smile diminished slightly as disappointment filled her countenance. Mina then forced the smile back on her lips. He could tell it was not a real smile.

"We'll get there," she replied.

"I hope so."

At that moment something stirred in his heart. Not a memory but an emotion. A strange mix of boldness and nervousness consumed him. Words had formed in his heart and filtered to his head but were blocked by the anticipation of embarrassment or possible rejection.

"I enjoyed our...discussion," he said. He felt his face burn and knew it turned red again as he spoke the words.

Mina's real smile returned. "We used to discuss matters a lot," she said. With a wink and a snap of the reins she drove her horse forward leaving him to ponder the meaning of her words. He felt an awkward grin form on his own lips. Quickly, he pulled the corners of his mouth down and cleared his throat and hoped none of the other men had seen it.

Ahead he saw the river he previously followed to Prador's estate. The party dismounted and looked around.

Benniah searched for signs of an ambush or anything that showed they were being followed. So far nothing but he remained alert. Something seemed different about this place. He just could not tell what it was.

Maybe after your welcome in Eden, you are just being paranoid, he thought.

"That could be," he answered himself out loud.

"What did you say, my lord?" asked the man nearest to him. Mina's small militia did not know his real identity or at least who Mina claimed he was. She introduced him as a general from some other kingdom he did not remember the name of.

"Nothing," he said quickly. The man bowed his head and returned to tending to his horse.

Benniah turned his attention to the forest as his horse drank from a pool of water on the riverbank. Something about the trees bothered him but he did not know what. A stiff wind blew and caused his cloak to fly into the air the way Trian Maras would swoosh his capes.

He noticed the tops of the trees and instantly knew what bothered him about the scene. All of the treetops moved with the wind. The illusion of the larger forest was gone. Something happened at the estate while he was in Eden. Dread devoured him momentarily as he pondered what the missing illusion meant. Something happened at Prador's estate and he had to find out what had transpired.

Benniah jumped back onto his horse and galloped off as quickly as possible. He didn't explain anything further. He did not bother to look to see if the others followed him. They would or they would not. At the moment he did not care. He had to check on Amber and Meldorn and Gerard.

The horse had barely stopped before he slid from the saddle. A moment later he entered the main building of the estate with his sword drawn.

The smell of death filled the air. The stench of decaying flesh filled his nose. He forced himself to not vomit. After a few moments, he noticed that the others had followed him. Mina whispered commands to the other men but Benniah did not hear her words. He was too focused on his surroundings.

A chill crawled down Benniah's spine as he walked the halls of Jonathon Prador's estate. Gone were the elaborate decorations. Paintings and beautifully woven tapestries once covered the walls but no longer hung in place. Except for a few tattered tapestries and several torches in sconces the walls were bare. Benniah spotted a rusted suit of armor.

The ornately carved furniture had been replaced with ordinary tables and chairs that would be found in any common home. It was as if Prador moved out and took anything of value with him. Benniah guessed the missing decorations were not taken but merely part of the previous illusion.

Benniah decided his previous mistrust of Jonathon Prador was now being earned. As much as the now sparse interior troubled Benniah, the silence troubled him more. No voices filled the halls. No servants moved around seeing to the day to day upkeep of the castle. Most important to him there were no signs of Amber, Meldorn or Gerard. Clearly Prador abandoned the estate but where did he go? And were his friends safe? He feared the worst for his friends.

He turned to see Mina and three of her men walk up to him. In a whisper she quickly explained she had left two men at the entrance with the horses. He ignored her and hurried forward to Prador's main receiving room. Here he discovered some answers but mostly more questions. Several of Prador's men lay dead on the stone floor.

"It must have been an assault," Mina said.

Benniah did not respond as he pondered the scene. Every man on the floor wore the colors of Jonathan Prador. Mina continued to speak but he continued to ignore her as he focused on the new question. Finally he heard her call his name.

"Prador double crossed us," he said flatly.

He provided no further explanation. He was certain that was the answer to the question. Something across the large room caught his eye. He stared at a dark spot on the far wall for a long time before he guessed what it was. He quickly crossed the room to take a closer look.

He heard Mina order the other men to search for survivors. He hoped they would find some. Mina ran up right behind him. As he inspected the dark spot closer, he realized he had guessed correctly. Someone leaned against the wall while badly bleeding. A trail of blood led down the adjacent hall.

"Would you care to explain why you think you were double crossed?" she asked.

"If a larger force attacked there should be more bodies and more carnage. Prador had a small army of his own, including about two dozen highly trained knights," he answered as they followed the trail of blood.

"So?"

"There should be dead men wearing other uniforms as well. All of the dead are Prador's men and there are only a handful of them."

Mina appeared to think about his explanation. "Perhaps it was a small attack and these men infiltrated the army to assassinate him or let in a larger army."

"Maybe, but why abandon a perfectly good fortress? Especially when Prador has the ability to create illusions that he could use to confuse an enemy. I would have stayed here. Prador definitely turned on us."

Benniah grew tired of the debate. He held up a hand to hush her before she spoke another word partly to end the debate but he also thought he heard something. He strained to listen carefully and continued forward.

The blood smears changed to bloody hand prints. With his sword drawn, Benniah crept forward. More bloody handprints appeared along the wall. They were spaced fairly evenly apart, at first. Slowly they appeared closer together. The hall ended with a trio of doors. One at the very end and one to the left and one to the right.

The door at the end of the hall opened easily. This room contained some buckets and brooms. The room on his left opened but only after he shoved on it with his shoulder. Stacks of what looked to be bags of corn and flour were in this room. The bloody hand prints ended at the door on the right side of the hall.

This door was locked. Trails of blood led beneath the door and hushed voices could be heard from behind it. Benniah returned to Mina. He leaned in close to whisper into her ear. Her hair smelled wonderful, like she crushed rose petals and covered her scalp with the juices. He had to focus.

"I hear voices coming from that room. Stand back," he whispered.

Their eyes met as he lingered near her for a moment too long. The corners of her mouth raised slightly then lowered as she attempted to resist a smile. Benniah saw the smile quickly jump on her lips for a moment. Something stirred inside him. Not a memory but the same familiarity with her he felt when she kissed hime before. The urge to kiss her came over him.

Now is not the time. He jerked backward and away from her, nearly losing his balance and crashing into the stone wall.

He motioned for Mina to step back. Reluctantly she did. He moved as far back across the hall as he could. He took two quick steps forward and kicked the door as hard as he could in the limited space. He gave a second and then a third kick. He silently prayed to Elyon. He remembered his mentor's words. Benniah closed his eyes and saw the door opening in his mind and spirit. He opened his eyes and spoke the command for the door to open. Wood splintered as the door exploded inward.

The bolt of a crossbow greeted him as it flew past his ear. The bolt missed its target but not by much. He felt the rush of air on the left side of his face and heard the slight whistle it made as it broke through the air. He heard the thud as it stuck into the door directly behind him.

A man sat with his back to the far wall and dropped the crossbow. He picked up a large hunting knife and a thin dagger. Benniah recognized the other man and rushed to his side. Whoever gave Captain Casser the beating, nearly beat him to death. His right eye had swollen nearly shut. Blood caked his nose and lips. The man would have likely died had Benniah not returned to the castle.

"What happened, Gerard?" Benniah asked. Mina stepped in and rushed to the other figure laying on the stone floor against the wall to their right. Gerard struggled to speak.

"Prador turned against us," he finally whispered. He winced as he attempted to adjust his posture. "After I returned from Midlothia, he attacked us and left us for dead."

A new face appeared in the door. Benniah lifted his sword. This new soldier wore the colors of Jonathan Prador. Benniah did not know him otherwise but he seemed to know Benniah.

"Lord Deweago, you're back," the young man said.

"Who are you?"

"My name is Lucas, sir." Lucas was young, not much older than twenty. Brown, wavy hair topped a slender body. His lightly tanned face likely resulted from recent prolonged outside guard duty. The young man's brown eyes took in the scene. He put his sword away and shouted for someone to bring water and bandages.

"What happened here?" Benniah demanded.

"I'm not sure, sir."

"Start from when Gerard arrived and tell me what you know," Benniah said allowing his anger to settle.

"Captain Casser returned two days ago. Yesterday a small envoy arrived, three centaurs, three elves and a half dozen well armed men."

"Centaurs?" Mina asked.

"Yes. One was mainly black and bigger than two war horses." Benniah looked to Mina. She seemed to recognize the description but only stood as two more men brought the water and some towels. They immediately went to the sides of the injured men. They gave them water and tended to their many wounds.

"What happened after the centaurs arrived?" she asked ignoring Benniah's look.

"I'm not sure. They were not here long. Maybe two hours later the envoy rode out with Lord Prador and just about every knight and soldier. There were four of us in the main gatehouse and no one summoned us. I was curious and sent one of the others to investigate. He found the dead men in the great hall."

"Where did Prador go?" Benniah asked as he stood.

The young man shrugged. "We tried to track them but all of the horses were gone. They rode south. We followed for as long as we could but with no horses or provisions we could not get very far."

"Where are the servants?" Mina asked.

"We just found them locked in another storage room. We let them return to their families in the nearby village", the young man replied.

Benniah remained silent for a moment while he tried to determine what Prador's next move would be. "He is going to the mines with Trian." He looked to Gerard. The man looked a little better but not by much. "Where are the weapons? Are they safe?"

"Prador's got them," he answered weakly and took another drink of water.

"What about the medallion?" Benniah asked. He did not want to push the man but he needed answers. Time was not on their side.

Gerard slowly shook his head. "He took that too and he has Amber."

Benniah caught a glimpse of the evil glare Mina gave him at the mention of Amber's name. He did not want to deal with jealousy now. Benniah threw his hands in the air and ran his fingers through his hair. Frustrated by the setback, he balled his fists up and slammed them against the stone wall.

"Deweago," another hoarse voice called out.

Benniah turned his attention to the other injured man in the room. He rushed to his side and knelt. Gently he turned his mentor to his back. Benniah barely recognized Meldorn's purple and swollen face. Blood covered his head and matted the old man's hair. Meldorn had been beaten so badly, Benniah was surprised the man survived as long as he did. The old man pointed up at him.

"You will know who you are when you know who you are. Then you will destroy the Najera," he whispered.

"Save your strength, Meldorn. Don't talk. Elyon, will heal you." Benniah said. He thought his friend was delirious. He spoke in riddles. Benniah prayed to Elyon and asked him to heal the old man and allow his friend to live. Tears streamed down Benniah's face as nothing seemed to change.

Meldorn tried to smile but his swollen lips only allowed for one corner of his mouth to raise. "No, He won't. Not this time." He took a labored breath. "It's okay. I've lived in this world longer than three hundred men."

"But—,"

"I am going to be with Elyon. Look to Him for all of your answers. You are greater than you know."

Meldorn finished his words and lay quietly a moment or two. The old man closed his eyes and despite the bruises, cuts and blood, he looked at peace. It was almost as if he were just resting. Benniah tried to fill the silence with words to encourage Meldorn to cling to life but only tears poured out. His mentor's breathing slowed and he took one last deep breathe. Meldorn passed into eternity to live with Elyon in paradise.

Benniah closed his eyes and began to sob. He did not know this man long but his loss hurt like Benniah thought it would if he lost his father.

Mina knelt next to him and wrapped her arms around him. He leaned his head against hers. He felt Mina stroke his cheek as he mourned his friend's death. He dropped his chin to chest and lowered his shoulders as he held the body of Meldorn. He prayed Elyon would return his mentor's life but in his spirit he knew that would not happen.

He sat holding Meldorn for a few minutes more. Somehow he knew he felt this kind of pain before.

chapter 8

After some rest and food, Gerard limped around. He still looked like he had taken a beating from an ogre but would live. Most of the servants stayed to help rather than return to the village. The dead were buried. Prayers were prayed for the families. Plans were made to carry on.

With the worst task completed, Benniah gave everyone willing to help tasks to prepare for the ride ahead. Some gathered food and water. Others searched for bows, arrows and other tools or weapons that may be useful. Prador and his men rode off the estate with every horse. Lucas took two men to the nearby village to purchase additional horses for the soldiers and men who would be riding with Benniah.

Gerard sat with Mina and Benniah at an outdoor table that overlooked their makeshift graveyard. Mina held

Benniah's hand. Benniah stared at the mound of dirt covering Meldorn's grave.

Prador will pay with his life.

Gerard's voice pulled his attention away from the grave marker. The captain began to explain exactly what happened at the estate.

"I rode hard from the fortress after you defeated the rider. I didn't stop for anything. I arrived in the middle of the night. Prador met me and insisted I give him the weapons for safe keeping."

"And you gave them to him without any questions?" Mina asked. Her tone bordered on accusatory.

Benniah understood why. Not long ago Casser served Trian Maras as his number one enforcer. Benniah believed the captain.

"Of course I did," Gerard answered. "We thought he was an ally. Jonathon Prador had been an outspoken opponent of Trian. We were always trying to find a way to make him look bad to the people. Trian could not move against Jonathon without the people rising up against him. That is how much of a good guy we believed him to be. "

"I would have given them to him too," Benniah said.

"I gave the medallion to Meldorn, just like you instructed me to."

Benniah ran his fingers through his hair. "How did they find out about the medallion?"

"I don't know. I was careful to give it to him in secret. In fact we were alone in his chamber when I gave it to him."

"What happened next?" Mina asked.

Gerard winced as he shifted in his seat. He took another drink from the cup in front of him. The liquid looked and smelled like swamp water. One of the servants wives mixed it for him and said it would help with his pain. He had to force the concoction down.

"I woke up the next day by being pulled from my bed. They started beating me right away. I tried to fight back and killed several of Prador's men but stopped when they started beating Meldorn. He just took each blow." Gerard stopped and cleared his throat. "He didn't give up the medallion. It just fell out of his robes. That is when they stopped."

Benniah sat silent imagining the pain his friend had endured to protect the medallion. Mina glanced at Benniah and then broke the silence.

"How did you get into the storage room?" she asked

"Everyone's attention was on the medallion. Then the big, dark centaur entered the room. I saw an opportunity and took it. We had enough strength to fight our way to the room. I locked us in. His men tried to get in but couldn't. Soon they just stopped trying. Everything was quiet until you showed up. I'm sorry I couldn't help Meldorn."

Benniah did not respond right away. He was not sure how to respond. Mina placed a hand on his shoulder. "You did what you could. I do not blame you. I blame Jonathon."

Benniah stood and walked to Meldorn's grave. Mina followed close behind. He sensed the other men around them but did not really hear or see any of them.

Everything became quiet and still like the world mourned Meldorn in this moment. Silently Benniah asked Elyon why he did not heal his mentor. He did not want to question Elyon, who would not likely provide him an answer. His God had not given him many answers yet. Benniah almost questioned if Elyon actually existed. Almost.

"Elyon works in his own ways," a familiar voice said from behind him.

Benniah did not want to hear anything about Elyon's mysterious ways right now. He turned to look at the source of the voice. "And yes, Elyon does exist."

The man that stared back at him had uncontrolled white hair. He wore a yellow robe whose style appeared to be from a different time yet the fabric looked new. The old man's face was cheerful, a little pale and seemed to have witnessed many winters yet held a sparkle in his blue eyes commonly seen in a young man.

"Prophet, I'm not in the mood for any of your riddles right now," Benniah replied.

The prophet did not say another word. He only stood there with the cheery smile on his face. Mina gasped. Benniah turned to see what was wrong with her. She simply stood with one hand covering her mouth. Her other hand extended as one finger pointed at him.

"You men are going to want to stand right here behind him," the prophet said stepping out of their way.

A moment later Benniah's world began to spin. He felt dizzy and sick to his stomach at the same time. Finally he dropped to one knee. Several sets of hands closed around his body.

A gentle hand slid up onto his shoulder and then onto his neck. He heard Mina speak but did not hear her words. The breath from her whisper warmed the back of his neck. An image rushed to him. Then another and another.

New images came to him one right after another in quick succession like he watched someone else's life pass in front of him. The images around him changed but each one contained the face of one man. Dark hair, lightening blue eyes, the face looked familiar. He quickly realized he did not see an illusion of the life of another man. He saw memories, his memories.

The images stopped on two older men. He knew them immediately. One man with brown hair streaked with grey. He wore a gold crown on his head. The other man wore grey robes and long grey hair. The man with the crown on his head was his father. The other was his uncle, Rufus. Blackness overtook him.

"Ethan, are you alright?" a soft voice asked through his darkened world. At first the sound came through muffled but quickly cleared as the question was repeated several times.

He blinked repeatedly until his normal vision returned. Mina, Gerard and the prophet stood over him and stared down at him. Concern filled Mina's face. Confusion and pain covered the face of Gerard. The cheerful smile still fully inhabited the prophet's. In the time the he had known the old prophet he always seemed to smile.

"What happened?" he asked trying to stand.

Mina spoke as the prophet held out one hand to help him up. "You turned to say something to the prophet and blacked out."

He looked at the three of them and recalled what just happened. "I looked at the prophet and everything started to spin. Then I woke up on the ground."

"What else do you remember?" the prophet asked.

Benniah paused. "What do you mean by that?," he said. The question seemed odd, even for the prophet.

The smile on the prophet's face changed. The corners of his mouth slid from friendly to mischievous. He looked like a child who had a secret. "What do you remember?"

"What kind of question is that?"

The prophet did not miss a beat. "What was your father's name?"

"Drew Lyons."

Mina let loose a short shriek. It was the same noise she used to make when they were children and someone gave her a gift. He quickly realized what happened. He remembered. His name was not Benniah Deweago. He was Ethan Lyons, King of Eden.

"Who are you?" the prophet asked.

"Ethan Lyons," he replied flatly.

Tears welled up in Mina's brown eyes and almost immediately spilled over and flowed like rivers down her cheeks. Ethan slid one hand behind her head and the other on her back as he pulled her close to him.

"I missed you," Ethan said.

"I'm so sorry that I tried to kill you," she whispered. He kissed her with the same passion she shared with him after she revealed she was Vanacore.

"I guess that means she's forgiven," Gerard said dryly.

Ethan gently wiped her tears from her cheeks after the kiss. He smiled and stared into her brown eyes for a long moment. "There is nothing to forgive," he said.

"Where do we go from here?" Gerard asked.

Ethan released his love's face. "Prador betrayed us. We need to find him, get those weapons back and save Amber," Ethan replied. He ignored Mina's glare when he mentioned the name of the princess of Tilibra again.

"What about Alaric?" Mina asked after giving up her moment of jealousy.

"Who?" Gerard asked wincing as he took a step closer to the king.

"Alaric is the sorcerer who put a spell on Ethan and took his place as King of Eden," Mina explained.

Ethan shook his head. "Alaric will have to wait. Right now we have a bigger issue. We need to get those weapons back," the king said.

"Do we go to the mines?" Gerard asked.

Ethan stepped away from those gathered around the grave to think. Though his memory had returned some details still evaded him.

Lord Elyon, give me wisdom, he prayed. Then the quiet voice spoke to his spirit. He remembered hearing it many times before. He knew this was Elyon directing him. The voice said two words. Trian Maras.

Ethan returned to the others. "Now that I know who I am. It's time Trian knows.

He ordered Mina to gather all of the men. Those who rode with them and Prador's remaining soldiers and servants. They were to meet at the main door with horses packed and ready to ride. With a quick nod of her head to acknowledge the command, she did as he asked.

The prophet remained with Ethan and Gerard. He prayed for the injured captain. Within seconds the bones broken by Prador's men returned to their rightful positions. The swelling around his eye disappeared along with the bruises and cuts on his face. He was still sore but could move around enough that he thought he could fight when called upon.

"Are you riding with us, Prophet?" Ethan asked as they walked to meet the others. The king pointed at the sword on the man's hip. He did not recall ever seeing the other with a sword before.

"No, Elyon has directed me to another destination. Our Lord's work is never complete."

The prophet walked to the line of graves. He stopped at Meldorn's. For the first time that Ethan could remember the prophet did not smile. He seemed to mourn for this man as well.

"Did you know Meldorn, prophet?" Ethan asked.

The old prophet nodded his head. "He was a good man. A good friend."

"That he was," Ethan replied. Silence lingered between the three men. "By the way, thanks for your help in Midlothia."

"Yes. The gate to the outer wall. It was really my pleasure. Especially to see the faces of those big, strong men." The prophet chuckled. "I think they are still puzzling about why that lever would not release."

Ethan could not stop himself from asking his next question. "How do you know Meldorn?"

The prophet stared into space a long moment. Ethan gave up on receiving an answer to his question right now. Perhaps someday. Then the wild haired prophet spoke.

"Many years ago, he and I were part of an order of warrior priests charged by Lord Elyon to teach his ways and care for and defend the defenseless." The prophet paused and seemed to reflect on the past. "But that was a long time ago and a story for another time."

"You mean another time when we do not have to defend the kingdoms of the world against a spoiled tyrant, a sorcerer and a trio of supernatural riders," Gerard said.

"Precisely," the prophet answered. His good natured smile returned and he walked by the king and his captain without another word.

Could it be? Meldorn and the prophet had both been Warriors of Elyon, Ethan thought. Quickly he dismissed the thought. The prophet was not going to share further details and the king needed to move if he were going to stop any of his enemies.

Mina and the others waited by the main entrance as instructed. He let the prophet and Gerard join the others and climbed to the third step to address his crowd.

"You men have pledged your allegiance to other leaders," he said. He paused a moment to look over the men and women who now stared up at him. "I have no intention of asking you to change those allegiances. I will ask you to consider riding with me to protect your families and to save your king. If you choose to walk away now, no one will think less of you. If you do stay, keep out of this battle. If you return to the battle against me, you will not be shown mercy as you will be siding with evil. Choose now."

Heads turned to look at each other. Most of the servants turned and walked away. Ethan expected nothing more from them. They were not soldiers.

Mina moved first to kneel. Gerard slowly knelt as well. One by one the men that rode with he and Mina were on their knees. Lucas and the other three soldiers Prador left behind joined the others. Two of the remaining servants looked at the women who stood at their sides. They hugged their wives and knelt. The women cried out and dropped to their knees in despair but the two men did not move. The remaining servants dispersed.

In a matter of minutes, only Ethan and the prophet remained standing. Ethan did not expect anyone to kneel, least of all the prophet, but appreciated the clear sign of the commitment these few were willing to make. Satisfied with the response, he gave his new army its first order. "Mount up."

chapter 9

Alaric Krollnoss had not been impersonating King Lyons for long. It had only been a few weeks since he made his appearance as the good king.

Some days felt like it had been an eternity. The last few days had been like that. Ulysses had disappeared while supposedly searching for Vanacore and the real King Lyons. Roland and the best trackers in the kingdom found no trace of the centaur, Vanacore or the real King Lyons. Tudyck and his wife continued to mope around the castle.

If they only knew the truth, he thought. He turned in front of the full length mirror in his chambers. Servants assisted him as he dressed.

Alaric did enjoy the perks that came with being king. Everyone jumped at his every command. Silver and gold filled the coffers and the wine never ran out. People revered him as their king. *Soon they would worship me as their god.* Alaric smiled. He liked the idea of being worshipped.

He dismissed the servants with a slight wave of his hand and a command to bring him more wine.

He admired the royal wardrobe. Lyons may have been his enemy but at least he dressed well. When he could not find something he liked to wear he decreed the tailors to make it and it was done. He stared at the mirror. The only part of his reflection he did not like to look at was Lyons' face staring back at him instead of his own.

That would change soon enough, he thought.

"Everyone will know my real face and fear me," Alaric said as he turned in front of the mirror to ensure all of his seams were straight.

A knock sounded on the heavy oak door. He made one final turn in the mirror. "Enter," he barked.

Kenneth entered first followed by Roland. Alaric put on his best smile for the pair.

"The riders have returned. The dais has been built to your specifications and people have begun to assemble in the field as directed," Kenneth reported.

The news pleased Alaric very much. Sometimes he liked being king. He really liked having things done at his every word. He began to think today would be a good day to be king.

"Is there anything else I can do for you, majesty?" Kenneth asked. He spoke with no emotion in his voice.

Alaric had grown tired of the continual moping both Tudyck and his wife had done since the death of their son. Neither of them had any idea of how important their child was to his plan. He did like the fact that they had gone from calling him by his friend's name to referring to him by more formal titles since their conversation after Vanacore's betrayal.

"That will be all," Alaric replied.

Kenneth turned to exit. Roland stood in his way and glared at the other man. Alaric shook his head and the bald man stepped aside. Kenneth returned the glare as he exited the room. Roland closed the door and walked to Alaric. The mercenary bowed his head briefly.

"Why can't I kill him?" he asked his master.

"Soon. Be patient, my friend," the sorcerer replied.

Roland slid a short throwing knife from one of the leather straps that always crossed his chest. His fingers lovingly caressed the entire blade. Alaric had always known that Roland was a little twisted and sick in the head but no one could doubt his effectiveness.

"Tudyck suspects something," Roland said.

Alaric shrugged. "He may, but it is of no concern. Everything is already set in motion. It will all be over soon. Then I will be the supreme ruler of all the kingdoms of the world. Only then can you kill him, his wife and his whole family."

"You do know that I have not killed anyone since we saved Tudyck's child from being sacrificed to the demon?"

"I am fully aware of when you last satisfied your bloodlust."

With a quick flick of his wrist Roland threw the knife and the blade stuck firmly in the closet door. "I need to kill something soon."

Alaric retrieved the knife. He walked back to the mercenary and handed the weapon to him.

"You will soon enough. In the meantime go into the forest and hunt some animals," Alaric said sternly.

He liked Roland a lot and did not want to dispose of the man as he had with countless others before. However, if Roland's bloodlust interfered with his plans then Alaric would not hesitate to do so.

The bald man hesitated but acknowledged the command with a nod. "Your brother and the centaur are waiting in your study."

"My brother?" The sorcerer's smile returned.

He liked this news even more. He had instructed his younger brother to only contact him if or when the weapons to kill and control the Najera had been recovered. "Excellent."

He wasted no more time in front of the mirror. The sorcerer rushed past Roland and out the door. He almost ran down the hall and down the stairs.

Alaric burst through the study door. Roland took up a post near the door and closed it after they entered. A younger man with black, widow-peaked hair and ice blue eyes sat behind the large wooden desk. A centaur covered in hair as black as midnight and about two times bigger than Ulysses stood on the far side of the room. Alaric could only guess how the large creature had been able to fit through the study's door.

A canvas bag lay on the desk. Alaric's heart pumped harder. He had waited a very long time for this moment. He had searched throughout all of the world for years for these weapons. For only a brief moment he wondered how his brother had come into possession of them but decided it did not matter. Trian Maras had obviously failed him and would be dealt with accordingly.

"Brother," Alaric said. "It is good to see you again."

"It is good to see you too." The man stood and walked around to the front of the desk. He held his arms open wide and embraced Alaric.

When they released the embrace, the sorcerer turned to the centaur. "Beserth, you have been quite useful."

"Thank you, majesty. I will remain useful as long as the gold and silver continue to come my way," the centaur said nonchalantly.

"Then I look forward to a long working relationship with you."

"As will I," the creature replied.

Alaric walked to his seat behind the desk. "You have made me very proud, Jonathan," Alaric said as he sat down. "I must admit that I didn't expect you to show up with these. Trian was supposed to obtain them as well as the jewel. How did you end up with them?"

Jonathan Prador smiled and said, "They walked through my front door."

"How so?"

"Two Rathuans showed up at my home, they had the medallion," Jonathan said as he pulled it from his pocket and handed it to his elder brother.

The jewel almost sparkled in the lamplight. Alaric felt the corners of his mouth twitch and begin to move up and into his wicked grin. Slowly he reached out and took it from Jonathan. The chain drooped over the side of his hand.

He ran his fingers across the jewel. It felt warm to the touch. He put the chain around his neck and gently lowered the medallion to his chest. He looked at his brother who also smiled wickedly at the sight. A glance to Beserth revealed the centaur truly only cared about getting paid as he watched uninterested, even bored.

Jonathan opened the canvas sack. He removed a broadsword and a double bladed battle axe. Alaric immediately twisted his face in confusion.

"The legends say there are four weapons. Where are the others?"

"I don't know, brother. These are all that were brought to me."

"What do you mean by 'brought to you'?"

"One of the Rathuans, a man called Benniah, and Trian's man, Captain Casser went on a mission to retrieve the weapons. Apparently Trian had them locked up in a tower. These two, are what Casser returned with."

Trian had betrayed me too.

Alaric felt his anger begin to swell inside. "What was the Rathuan's name again?"

"Benniah Deweago," his brother replied meekly.

With his fists clenched, Alaric screamed at the top of his lungs. The evil sound attracted the attention of a passing guard who opened the door to check on the king. As soon as the guard peeked inside, Roland shoved him out and slammed the door shut.

"What's wrong, Alaric?" Jonathan asked.

"Benniah is Ethan Lyons. If he knows about the Najera then my plan could be in jeopardy."

"Why?"

"Because he is a warrior of Elyon," Alaric answered through bared teeth. "He is the one being who could destroy the Najera without these weapons."

Beserth huffed and snorted, finally sounding interested in the conversation. "The Warrior of Elyon is as much of a myth as Elyon is. They simply do not exist."

"Whether you believe it or not, they do exist and he is out there on the loose," Alaric replied.

"I do not understand. Casser said the Rathuan was headed here to see you. If he was that much of a threat then why didn't you lock him in the dungeon?"

Jonathan stepped back because of his brother's glare. "I did but he escaped!"

Alaric breathed deep to calm himself. He wanted to shoot lightening through each of them right now. *That spell has too much preparation, it would take too long.*

He unclenched his fists and sat down at his desk instead. He placed his elbows on the desk and put his head in his hands as he tried to compose himself. Finally he sat back and ran his fingers through his hair.

"He needs to be destroyed."

"How do you destroy the indestructible?" Beserth asked with a cocky grin. "After all, the legends indicate that a Warrior of Elyon is invincible."

Alaric returned the grin. "He does not know who he is. The strength of the warrior comes from his faith in Elyon. He can't have faith in what he does not know. Find him and kill him."

"What about Trian Maras?" Beserth asked. "He knows who you are."

Alaric thought for a moment. Now that he had the weapons and the medallion, he no longer needed Trian. The man had also proven to be disloyal to him. "Kill him."

The centaur bowed his head respectfully. "He also contracted my services and still owes me a portion of the debt. Once I have been paid in full, I will gladly kill him for you."

Alaric could not begrudge anyone for wanting to get paid for services so he decided to let Beserth handle Trian his way. He looked to Roland who stood silently at his post.

"Pay the centaur what we owe him and add another thousand gold pieces for down payment on Trian and Lyons' heads." Alaric looked up into the eyes of the gigantic centaur. "You will receive another four thousand when I have proof they are both dead."

"Trian I'll kill for free. I will bring you the head of your enemy," Beserth replied.

The sorcerer turned back to Roland, "Make accommodations for my brother and make sure Beserth is escorted safely out of the castle. He cannot be seen by anyone."

Roland bowed and turned to leave. The black centaur and Jonathan followed. Alaric stared at the weapons on the desk for a long time. His triumph neared. Soon he would control an invincible army and no one would be able to stop him. Not Ethan Lyons or an army of Elyon's warriors. Alaric doubted that Elyon himself would be able to stop him.

He picked up the slender sword. It had a small gold hilt and could be wielded with one hand. Balanced and light, he did not expect this type of weapon to be in the arsenal. He envisioned a long two-handed broadsword.

He gently placed the blade back onto the desk and turned his attention to the medallion. He lifted the chain from around his neck and stared into the jewel. Somehow he sensed the power held within. He felt his wicked smile cross his lips again. The power felt so good to him.

Something strange caught his eye. At first he thought he saw a reflection of light but then determined it was not a reflection. Slowly, what seemed to be a mist swirled inside the gem. As the mist cleared the sorcerer saw a face. It looked like a man with orange skin thinly stretched over his skull. The gaunt face returned Alaric's evil grin. The face startled him at first but the quick fright fell away as his confidence in his ultimate victory grew.

chapter 10

The sun had risen on the appointed day. The crowds had gathered, everything had been set as he had commanded. Alaric's magic could do a lot and he would use it today but the miracle he proposed to do could not be duplicated with any spell he had ever learned. One time he had witnessed someone being raised from the dead. The prophet had done that the night they saved the Tudyck woman and child. Perhaps Elyon was the only true power in the world.

He shook his head to no one. *No,* he thought. *Once I control the Najera rider known as Death, I will control his power. I will have ultimate power over life and death.*

He stood in the shelter that had been built for him to stay in. He arrived last night and slept in a fairly comfortable bed. He rose early and watched as the crowds gathered. Slowly at first but by evening the field was nearly full.

Many of the people stayed out in the fields under canvas shelters. Others slept under the open skies with only a blanket to cover them. The richer nobles, able to afford better shelters, erected small buildings covered in animal hides. These buildings were similar to what he stayed in.

Meanwhile, the poor families huddled together under one or two blankets, if they were lucky. Some had only the clothes on their backs to keep them warm. As king, Alaric expected none of the shelters to be more extravagant than his. Roland ensured the king's shelter for the evening was the grandest of them all.

A knock sounded on the door and a servant entered at the king's command. The man carried a full length mirror. Alaric stood in front of the mirror the man held. He had to look his best today when he revealed all to the people. Everything fit perfectly. The royal tailors took two days but they made the finest shirt, pants and tunic for him. The only thing that made the clothes better was when he put them on.

Someone else knocked on his chamber door as he smoothed wrinkles out of his silk pants. "Enter," he answered.

Roland entered the room. Alaric commanded the servant to leave. Obediently the servant set the mirror down and left the two men alone.

"You look very regal today, majesty," Roland said with a bow. The mercenary wore nicer clothes than normal. Alaric had asked the other to dress more appropriately as a representative of the king. He still wore the knives on the straps across his chest.

"Excellant."

"The people wait for the appearance of their king."

"How many?" the fake king asked adjusting his crown.

"Roughly twenty thousand souls, including children, are present to witness the miracles you will bring about today," the bald mercenary reported.

Alaric twisted his face in disgust. He wanted more people to witness this day. He needed more people to witness what he planned to do.

"I am sure word will spread quickly," Roland said as if he read his master's thoughts.

Alaric hated when people tried to appease his ego by stating the obvious. "Word *will* spread quickly. Soon all of Eden and beyond will know and they all will bow to me."

"And if they won't bow?" Roland asked.

Alaric waited to give the answer. He wanted Roland to appreciate it. "Then I unleash my demon."

He thought the mercenary would like that answer. The lift in the other's face seemed to verify that fact. "Well, majesty, shall we make history?"

Alaric allowed Roland to exit first. The king followed close behind him. Alaric had waited for this day for a long time. The mix of emotions that churned inside of him came as a surprise.

When he began his conquests nearly a decade ago he had envisioned both of his brothers ruling at his side. Xestes was never one for patience. His greed led to his demise and ended Alaric's vision of a glorious future with the three of them ruling the world.

He pushed the thought aside and stepped onto the dais. Chatter in the crowd ceased. A human wave rippled through the gathering as the people knelt at the king's arrival. He basked in the adoration of the thousands of people in the field. He could not help but smile.

He felt a surge of energy envelope his body as the silence broke into cheers. A chant of 'long live the king' broke out. He soaked it in until he realized the people cheered for Ethan Lyons and not for Alaric Krollnoss.

The smile momentarily changed to a sneer at the thought. *Stay in character,* he thought as he forced the smile to return.

He allowed the chanting to continue for several moments longer. He waved to the crowd and even pointed directly at a few individuals to make them feel important. He would not remember their faces in an hour but people liked to feel special. He had learned this lesson over the course of his conquests. Often he made someone feel special or important as the first step in manipulating them.

The noise had died down to the point where he could take control. He raised his hands for quiet. It took longer than he liked but every voice silenced. The field became very still. No one moved, not even the children. Even the wind seemed to sense the history about to be made as it ceased when Alaric stepped to the edge of the platform.

Alaric studied the people's faces. Some were old and wrinkled and not likely to survive too many more winters. These people did not matter to him. They would be dead soon. If time or disease did not take them then their stubbornness about keeping to their old ways would see them as a victim to Roland's blades.

Some faces were older but still strong. They likely had at least one grown child. They would be tough to win over and he would likely have to put many of their numbers to death, not that the bloodthirsty mercenary would mind.

Then there were the younger faces among the congregation. Young men and women yearning to break away from the traditions of their parents. They would be easy to turn into his followers. He would need them and he knew they would come to him in droves.

He desired the children most. He knew if he could win the hearts of the children he would be worshipped for generations to come. They would grow up believing he was Elyon and would teach their children and their children's children to worship him alone.

"Citizens of Eden, today I come to you as your king. I bring to you a message of hope and peace." He paused allowing the people to hang on to his words. "The one true God, Elyon, has given a message to me. You will be the first to hear it. You will be the first to experience an awakening of the spirit like no other time in history. Today Elyon unites all people under his banner of love and peace."

Murmurs began to rumble through the crowd. Alaric expected such a doubtful reaction from the people but as always he came prepared. He motioned for Roland who immediately and dutifully approached the sorcerer.

"Are they ready?" Alaric asked. Roland nodded. "Good, then bring them up."

Alaric had planted several people in the front of the audience. Two of them leaned on canes and crutches to walk while another had one arm in a sling. The last man had a bloodied bandage on his head. All of the injuries were faked.

They would all be used to show the miraculous power that Elyon had granted to him. The people walked, staggered and limped across the platform and stood in a single line behind him and faced the crowd.

"People of Eden, the Lord Elyon has appointed me as his messenger to all kingdoms. As a demonstration of his appointment and his power given to me miracles are about to be performed."

The murmurs changed into raised voices. Many of the older people shouted their disapproval of his statement. Many people in Eden worshipped their own god. Some worshipped Elyon but there were many other gods worshipped in the temples around the kingdom. Alaric believed either his demonstrations today or his enforcement would change that practice. Again he raised his hands for quiet.

He looked at the first person in the line. A young man with his arm in a sling. "Step forward, young man."

The man did as he was asked. Alaric spoke a few words in an obscure dead language then pulled the sling off of the man's arm. The young man acted surprised and started waving the injured limb in the air.

Alaric stepped up to the two men faking leg injuries. Again he spoke the words and the men threw down their cane and crutches. They began to run and jump around. Finally he stopped in front of the man with the bloody bandage on his head. The blood was only for theatrics. There was no wound underneath the bandage but the people did not know that. Alaric removed the bandage to show no wound.

People in the congregation raised their voices again, skeptical of the show he had already put on. They should be skeptical, charlatans roamed the countryside showing off cheap tricks such as these.

He expected this response and prepared properly. It was time for the finale. Again he raised his hands for quiet. This time the voices did not heed the request.

He spoke again and this time raised his voice with the aid of a few tricks he had learned. He called for silence. His voice echoed in the distance and the uneasy stillness returned to the field. He spoke again after the last echo sounded back at him.

"Elyon *has* appointed me his messenger. You *will* believe," Alaric said.

Roland carried a dirty bundle out to Alaric. Another servant led Kenneth and Krysta onto the dais as well.

"What are you doing?" Kenneth asked in a whisper.

"Peace, my friend, " Alaric whispered back. He turned and took the bundle from Roland.

"Ethan—," Kenneth started.

Alaric ignored Tudyck as he addressed the gathering again. "Several days ago my good friends lost their son to the cold, icy fingers of death." He paused for dramatic effect. The people hung onto every word. He could not make a mistake now.

Get ready for the big finish, he thought.

"I have struck an accord with Elyon. I agreed to be his representative to all people if he would return their child to them."

He handed the bundle to Krysta. She unwrapped the bundle quickly and carefully. Her eyes lit up as she saw the child. He was healthy and moving. In timing that Alaric wished he could have controlled, the baby smiled at her.

Tears began to stream down her cheeks. Alaric could not have scripted it any better.

"Is this your son?" he asked Kenneth placing a hand on the man's shoulder in a way that as if he truly cared.

Tudyck's face froze at first, stunned at the sight of his child living and breathing and wiggling in the arms of his mother.

"Yes, but why now?" Kenneth asked.

His face changed and betrayed his emotions. The look on his face no longer reflected the pure joy of his wife's. Tudyck's face contained questions. Alaric realized that Kenneth would indeed be trouble and therefore would need to be eliminated.

The sorcerer ignored the question and spoke to the people. "This miracle is a sign of Elyon's covenant. He will bless those who worship him through me. He is also a jealous god and has instructed me to put to death all those who refuse to worship him."

He paused again to allow the words to take full affect as murmurs started up again. He glanced at Kenneth who glared back at him.

"In the coming days riders will come to your towns and villages. You will be given a choice. Serve me and Elyon or die."

He did not wait for any protests to begin. He exited the dais leaving a clearly upset Kenneth there with his ecstatic wife and living child.

chapter 11

Alaric wasted no time, as soon as he left the gathering riders were dispatched. The decree had been made. These men would enforce the new law of the land. The riders would go to the farthest reaches of the kingdom. They would return with lists containing the names of those who confirmed their worship of him or prisoners to be executed.

He hoped that the lists contained more names than the number of prisoners returned. He did not want to kill a large number of people, he craved the worshippers. On the other hand he would kill as many as needed to make his point clear.

He sat on the throne and began accepting pledges right away. No one had yet refused to bow and accept him as their god. Pleased with the initial response, he accepted each one and blessed them as they rose.

They bowed because they truly thought Elyon had embodied his flesh or because they feared for their lives. The reason for their worship did not matter to him.

His plan called for Eden to fully worship him and once the riders had returned with their prisoners and the executions completed, he would expand his influence using Elyon's name. He smiled at his perfect plan.

All that was left to do was for Beserth to eliminate the real Ethan Lyons. Alaric had the utmost confidence in the centaur's ability to kill the man. The centaur had already proven most useful several times in this campaign. The sorcerer blessed another member of the castle staff as she stood back up before him.

Unexpectedly another name sprang to mind. Ulysses was still missing. He still worked on gathering clues to locate Lyons and Vanacore. He had not yet returned. He too worshipped Elyon as a zealot. He would not be easy to convince. The sorcerer dismissed the thought as quickly as it had come to him. *If the centaur refused to bow he would suffer the same fate as any other*, he thought.

The day's events tore Kenneth to pieces. Joy from having his son returned to him again filled his heart. Yet questions about why Elyon allowed his death to begin with and then seemed to resurrect the baby days later still filled his spirit. Suspicion of Ethan consumed his mind now more than ever before.

The king's recent actions worried him. The way he treated those who were supposed to be his friends bothered him. Today's announcement that people were to worship him as they would Elyon only confirmed his suspicions. He did not know who the king was but was now certain he was not his childhood friend.

Kenneth did not know Elyon like Ethan did but he knew Elyon did not allow worship of other gods. He even remembered Ethan saying Elyon was a jealous god. He also knew Ethan would not claim to be Elyon or Elyon's messenger. As far as Ethan was concerned the wild haired prophet who always showed up unexpectedly was Elyon's messenger.

When he accepted that the king was not really Ethan, some things began to make sense. Why the king chose Roland and Vanacore as advisors over he and Atherton made sense. He now understood the obsession with formal titles and the lack of compassion when they found his son had died. He had not yet shared his concerns with Krysta. She rested with their son. She deserved the peace and quiet with the baby and he would let her have it.

He bit into a crisp apple. As he chewed juices sloshed around his mouth and down his throat. Suddenly a revelation struck him. "He lied," Kenneth said with his mouth full to no one.

He remembered the elves. Kiat and his bodyguards had died in the battle to save Krysta and his son from the demon, Charax. The impostor said that Elyon would not resurrect them but the prophet did raise them from the dead with Elyon's power. The fake king did not have power from Elyon. He could not have because if he did he would have called the Tulchin elves back from paradise on Elyon's authority.

Kenneth's temper flared at his next thought. He threw the apple and it exploded against the far wall, leaving splattered juice and pieces on the stone. He turned to wake Krysta. He had no choice but to tell her now. He was certain that this fake king had stolen their baby and faked his death just to be able to show he had power.

A knock on the door interrupted his march to the bed chamber. The knock sounded a second time. "Lord Tudyck, the king requests your family's presence," the voice said through the wooden door.

Kenneth opened it. A lanky soldier in chain mail and helmet two sizes too big for him stood on the other side. "I need a moment. Krysta and the baby are sleeping. I'll wake them," he said. The soldier nodded.

Kenneth rushed to the bed. Krysta laid on her side, eyes wide open. She stared at Olin and stroked his face. They named the boy after their fathers shortly after their return from the battle with Charax. Olin Vaughn Tudyck slept peacefully on his back. It was a shame they would have to wake him.

"We are being summoned," he said. He shifted his weight from one foot to the other. "We can't bow down to him and worship him."

Krysta wrapped the blanket around Olin. "Don't be silly. Elyon worked through Ethan to return Olin to us."

She picked up the baby and moved to the door. Kenneth followed close behind.

"That's just it. The king is not Ethan."

She stopped. "What are you talking about? If that is not Ethan then who is he?"

Her question was a valid one. He lowered his eyes.

"I don't know," he admitted. "But I don't believe that Olin was dead. I think this impostor switched him with another child."

"Who would do such a thing?" Krysta asked. A stern glare replaced her smile.

He knew she would require more convincing proof. The soldier knocked again. Kenneth had run out of time. He knew what he had to do. He knew that Krysta would not understand.

Elyon please honor my faith and protect my family, he silently prayed.

Krysta followed the soldier into the hall. Kenneth followed his wife. He dreaded what was to come next. It was not execution he dreaded but leaving his wife and son alone. He knew Krysta would not understand. He just hoped he would have a chance to explain everything to her.

They stopped in front of the impostor who sat on Ethan's throne. The man wore Ethan's finest clothes. He had the same face as his friend, the same dark hair. Even his lightening blue eyes matched Ethan's. Kenneth did not know how this man managed it but he looked like the king. He sounded like the king, yet Kenneth knew this man was not Ethan.

Atherton also stood in front of the man. One of the herald's rattled off an oath, they were supposed to repeat and agree to. Kenneth heard the man's voice but the words came through as if he spoke a foreign language. He stared at the impostor. His eyes locked with the other man's. The smile never changed.

Kenneth almost wished he had a sword or a crossbow. He would use it right now. He set aside thoughts of killing the fake king. He realized it would do them no good because then they would lose their chance at finding the real Ethan. Kenneth needed to find his friend. Ethan, the real Ethan would be the only one who could truly unmask this man.

The face of the man who claimed to be his friend changed. The friendly smile disappeared. He did not look angry but something changed his disposition. Kenneth looked all around to see what had caused the change. He saw Krysta kneeling with the baby cradled in her arms. She whispered his name several times.

The herald's voice brought him to his senses.

"Lord Tudyck, do you solemnly swear?" The man asked.

Kenneth looked at Krysta. He could already see the tears welling up in her eyes.

"I love you," he said.

"Do you swear?" asked the herald.

Roland took a step forward. He looked like a wolf ready to pounce. Everyone waited for his response.

Kenneth stood straighter and defiant. "I cannot," he replied.

"Neither can I," said Atherton.

At least I'll be in good company facing the gallows, Kenneth thought.

The impostor's face became angry. For just a moment something changed. Ethan's face was replaced by another. The eyes, nose and mainly the widow's peaked hair all appeared for a blink of an eye. The face seemed oddly familiar. In fact, if he had not known better he swore he saw the face of Xestes Krollnoss with streaks of grey in his black hair.

The man stood. He pointed his finger at Kenneth. "You will bow or die."

His voice was calm and steady but the words were laced with anger like an arrowhead dipped in poison.

"No," Kenneth said.

Tears broke free from Krysta's eyes and rolled down her cheeks. "Please, Kenneth, just swear. Please, don't do this."

The baby began to cry. Kenneth's heart broke at the sound of his son. His wife continued to plead with him. He had to make a stand. This was not his friend. It was not of Elyon.

He had to let the world know. His heavy heart almost made him speak the words. What good could he do if he was dead? If he spoke the words, at least he could buy some time to expose this man and find the real Ethan.

Kenneth looked at his wife. Her green eyes were blurred by tears. "This is not Ethan. This man is a liar," he said.

"Take them away," the fake king said.

Krysta's cries grew louder as the guards escorted him down the hall to the dungeon. He closed his eyes and tried to ignore them. In his spirit, he knew this is what Elyon really wanted from him.

chapter 12

Kenneth sat in the dark with his back against the stone wall. He leaned his head back against the stone. He heard Atherton as the guardian paced the the large cell they shared.

Neither of them had been shackled or chained in any way. This surprised him. He thought the impostor would be sure to lock them in the most secure manner possible after the escape of the other prisoner and Vanacore.

They had not been thrown into the inner prison in the dungeon. A small barred window allowed some fresh air into the cell. Through the space in the wall, light from the stars could be seen as well. Although tonight the clouds masked much of that light.

Kenneth assumed Atherton paced the floor, not out of fear of death, but because he just could not sit still and wait.

Kenneth could not wait either. All he could think about though was his family. Krysta had been devastated by his decision to take a stand. The thought that Olin would grow up without his father brought tears to his eyes.

He knew that feeling and swore long ago if he had a child he would do everything in his power to ensure that did not happen. His next thought really frightened him.

Not only would Olin grow up without his father, he would grow up believing this imposter was Elyon. Silently he prayed for Krysta's soul and for Olin's too. He prayed Elyon would stop this imposter. He prayed Elyon would spare his life and Atherton's.

He knew the real Elyon could prevent his execution. He just was not sure the Lord of All would. Kenneth had only just begun to acknowledge Elyon as his God.

Ethan, the real King Lyons, had followed the deity for a number of years. Kenneth had witnessed several times when Elyon came to the rescue of his friend. He hoped Elyon would rescue him this time but understood if rescue did not come.

Kenneth decided either way he would follow Elyon with whatever time he had left. It did not matter if he had a few hours or a few decades. Kenneth had turned his life over to Elyon. He hoped that word would get to Ethan just so his friend would know about his change.

The scrape of the key in the lock on the door interrupted his thoughts. The door opened. The light from the torches in the hall lit up the room. Several guards filed in. Roland followed them. Krysta entered last.

"You have a visitor," the bald man said with his wolfish grin. He let Krysta pass and then he exited. The guards however remained.

"Kenneth," Krysta said running to him. He stood and she wrapped her arms around his neck and kissed him. The long soft kiss warmed his heart. Holding her in his arms again tempted him to recant and bow to the fake king's claim. Again he thought he could do more alive than dead.

Reluctantly he pulled away from her kiss but still held her in his arms. Her arms remained around his neck. "Why are you here?" he asked.

"Ethan gave me one more opportunity to convince you to swear to him. Please, just do it."

He looked down and shook his head. "I can't."

Fresh tears spilled down her face. "What about me? What about Olin? Don't you love us?"

Her question stung his heart and pierced his soul. *How could she think that?*, he thought. He knew the answer to his question.

He had the power to change the situation. The impostor gave him several chances already to change his mind. If he recanted now, something told him he would likely end up with the same fate, just not at the end of a noose.

"Of course, I love you both. I just can't do what he is asking."

"He raised Olin from the dead," she said.

Her eyes filled with new tears as they silently begged him to change his mind. His heart pounded in his chest. The temptation to recant and bow to the imposter grew. He wanted to remain with her and raise his son. Elyon would understand.

Kenneth would not give in now. "No, he didn't raise Olin from the dead. I don't know how but he deceived everyone. Somehow he switched our child with a dead one. He let us grieve and mourn thinking our son was dead. All while he hid our child from us."

She released her grip from him and pulled back. He let her go.

"I don't understand. Why would Ethan do that to you? You are his best friend."

"He's not Ethan," Kenneth replied.

She looked at him like she still did not believe him.

"Let's say I believe you. How does getting yourself executed help stop him?"

Her tone held a bitter edge to it. The tears temporarily disappeared replaced by anger. On more than one occasion he had been subject to her temper. Most of the time he deserved her wrath. Now was not the time to argue.

"Listen to yourself. Would Ethan Lyons really execute anyone? Especially two of his most trusted friends."

Krysta's face softened. He thought he had gotten through to her. Maybe she finally understood. She looked him directly in the eyes.

"You didn't answer my question."

"I know." He paused. He really did understand her point and wanted her to understand him. "I couldn't do anything. You are right but if I gave in I could not live with myself. Elyon will take care of this impostor. No matter what happens to me, Elyon will take care of you and Olin as well."

The tears began again. She rushed to him. Her body collided with his briefly knocking his breath away. They wrapped their arms around each other. She began to sob.

"Please don't do this," she whispered.

Kenneth kissed her on the top of her fiery head. "I don't have a choice. Someone has to stand up to this man."

"Time's up," Roland said as he entered the cell. "This is your last chance. What is your answer?"

Kenneth looked Krysta in her beautiful green eyes. Her gaze still pleaded with him. He glared at the mercenary. "No."

Roland's predatory grin returned. He looked at Atherton. "And what about you?"

Atherton looked down at the bald man, being a foot taller than the mercenary. "No."

Roland flipped his head toward the door and one of the guards took Krysta by the arm. She resisted and Kenneth could tell she was thinking about fighting back. She could handle herself but she needed to not wind up in prison too. Kenneth pushed the guard away from his wife. He pulled her in close and kissed her one last time.

"Go to Olin. Don't fight them. Everything will be okay."

She released him. "I love you," she said then turned.

The guard escorted Krysta out of the room. She screamed her protest as she went.

Kenneth closed his eyes to stop from crying himself. He heard her cries from down the hall. Every one of her cries challenged his fortitude. Every time she yelled his name, his heart screamed for him to give up and surrender.

He was tempted. Perhaps if he did and gave the impostor no further trouble they would be allowed to live in exile. They would not be in Eden but they would be together.

Right after thoughts of exile another voice came to him. A quiet soft voice spoke. It spoke to his spirit. *Peace*, it said. With only one word the storm in his mind and soul ceased. Peace took control just as it had before when he heard this voice after he thought Olin was dead.

Roland's voice made him open his eyes. "I'm looking forward to cutting your heads off."

Kenneth stood straight. A boldness like he had never felt before filled him. He looked the other in the eye. "I look forward to doing the same to you."

The bald man chuckled. "I'd like to see that."

He gave the command and another guard tied the prisoner's hands in front of them. The guards led Kenneth and Atherton out of the dungeon.

Kenneth noticed the servants as they passed through the castle. Most of them shot angry looks at the prisoners and made slashing motions across their throats. The number of people who seemed angry really surprised Kenneth.

How could so many people be deceived?

He passed a cook that he knew since he was a child growing up in the castle. Streaks glistened down her cheeks. She made no effort to hide her tears. She had watched him and Ethan grow up together. He hoped one day she would learn the truth. He nodded to her, a small gesture to reassure her. She gave a small wave in response.

The guard behind him pushed him, knocking him slightly off balance. Kenneth stumbled but did not fall.

"Keep moving," the man said pushing him again.

Out in the courtyard torches lined a path from the main door and out through the gate. The trail of torches led to a platform just outside the castle walls.

A crowd had gathered to watch Roland remove the heads of the first two unbelievers. The mob shouted insults and hissed at them as he and Atherton passed. Rotten fruit flew through the air. Clumps of dirt thrown at him smashed into Kenneth's body.

Something soft splatted against the side of Kenneth's face. As he wiped it off he nearly vomited. Someone had thrown horse dung at him. He could not stand the smell especially so close to his nose. He dropped the clumps onto the ground and used his sleeve to wipe the rest off of his head.

Kenneth glanced back and took a punch to the head for his effort. A guard followed Kenneth. Behind him stood Atherton. Roland followed the entire line. Kenneth did not like the twisted joy the bald man took in the idea of being their executioner. He hoped Roland would do them the courtesy of making the cut clean.

The number of people assembled to watch the execution was far less than the number gathered to witness the so called miracle earlier. He climbed the stairs to the platform.

Krysta stood near the front of the crowd. Tears still rolled down her cheeks but the screaming had stopped. He guessed it would begin again in just a few moments. He wondered if she could even see him through the tears in her eyes.

The fake king climbed the steps to the platform. Briefly their eyes locked. Kenneth tried to look defiant. He did not want this man to see any fear or hesitation in his eyes. The other man released the gaze as he turned to address the mob.

"Let it be known to people everywhere the punishment for disobedience is death," he said.

He faced the prisoners. The wicked smile the man flashed looked like the one Ethan hated from Xestes Krollnoss. It only confirmed to Kenneth that he was right about this man. Hands on each of Kenneth's shoulders held him in place while the fake king stood in front of him.

"Any last words?" he asked Kenneth.

"You won't get away with this," Kenneth replied through gritted teeth.

The other leaned in close. "I already have." He raised a medallion he wore around his neck. "If Roland does not find your friend then the Najera will. Either way you will all be dead and no one will be able to stop me." He let the jewel drop back to his chest.

Kenneth struggled against those who held him. The man just confessed to him. Kenneth received a slap to the back of the head and stopped his struggle.

"Elyon will stop you," Kenneth shouted.

The fake king's smile changed. It began to look like the mouth of a viper. "Off with their heads!"

The crowd erupted at the command. The impostor descended the stairs. Kenneth glanced back to his wife. He thought he saw the wild-haired prophet. The man who truly spoke for Elyon. Another familiar looking man stood on her opposite side.

"Start with the big one," Roland commanded.

The four guards surrounding Atherton pushed him forward. The former guardian did not speak a word. He took the insults and fruit thrown his way. Two of the guards punched him in the lower back. A third pounded him in the gut. Atherton doubled over. He did not fall to his knees.

"Get him down!" shouted Roland as he anxiously spun the shaft of the executioner's axe in his hands. The fourth guard kicked Atherton behind the knee. The blow took the guardian down.

The first guard punched Atherton in the face and another bashed him in the back of the head. Kenneth struggled to help his friend but received another hit to the head. The crowd gasped and winced with each blow but then cheered and shouted for the prisoners to die.

As Kenneth refocused his eyes after the retaliation he received, he saw that Krysta no longer stood in front of the platform. Relief came over him. He did not want her last memory of him to be his head bouncing to the ground. Another blow struck him on the right side of his head.

"You'll get your turn soon enough," the guard behind him said.

Kenneth did not reply but could not understand why these guards were so brutal. All of the palace guards knew him. When his vision cleared again he understood. These men were not normal palace guards. They were mercenaries. Likely friends of Roland Melkin.

One of the four men who surrounded Atherton forced the guardian's head onto the stone. Another grabbed the hair that covered his neck and pulled it forward to give Roland a clean area to strike the axe. They laughed and joked as they did. Kenneth did not understand how his friend remained so calm with death only a heartbeat away.

Kenneth's hands shook and his heart threatened to burst from his chest. He resolved not to lose his dignity or give Roland the satisfaction of seeing fear cross his face.

"There's no reason to get blood all over that fancy white cloak," Roland said.

The gathered crowd's cry for blood grew louder as they chanted, "Off with his head!"

Kenneth knew many of theses people personally and could not understand why they craved blood so much. Especially his blood.

"Off with his head!"

The chant grew louder as more voices joined the chorus. A clod of dirt stung Kenneth's chest. He ducked as rocks began to fly. He raised his bound hands to block the projectiles. From the corner of his eye he saw one of the guards peel off Atherton's cloak.

No one expected the light, least of all Kenneth. Brilliant white light shone all around. Atherton's wings expanded. The guard to his right was knocked off of the platform. Atherton stood to his full height despite the grip the men holding him had on his body.

The man holding Atherton's long mane fell back into the crowd. He slammed his bound fists against the chest of the guard to his left. Atherton broke his the ropes that bound his hands simply by jerking his hands apart. He followed that with a quick turn and front kick to the fourth man knocking him off the platform as well.

The two men holding Kenneth moved to assist their comrades. Atherton dispatched them both first by dodging the first man's punch. The second guard swung a fist at the guardian. Atherton redirected the blow. Instead of striking the guardian the man's fist landed on the jaw of the guard next to him. Atherton threw a right cross of his own knocking the guard out. The people in the crowd ran in every direction. Their scattering thwarted attempts of additional guards to reach the platform.

Roland paid no attention to Kenneth as he barked orders to his men about how to stop the guardian. He screamed for reinforcements.

Kenneth took advantage of the confusion. He kicked the bald man in the side of his left knee. The axe fell from his hands as Roland dropped to his knees. Kenneth slammed the heels of his still bound fists onto the other man's back.

He kicked the side of the mercenary's head. Roland only seemed to get angry but was slow in standing back up. Kenneth reached for and pulled one of the blades that Roland wore on the straps across his chest. Even with his hands tied together, Kenneth held a good grasp on the hilt of the knife. He attacked with a downward slice at Roland's throat.

A pair of hands grabbed him from behind and pulled him back. The action caused him to miss Roland's exposed neck and instead slash his head and cheek. Kenneth began to rise. His feet lifted off of the platform and he ascended above the chaotic scene below.

chapter 13

Kenneth watched in awe as the field and the chaos it contained grew smaller. For a moment he thought he was having an out of body experience. Or perhaps he had somehow been killed in the struggle and was floating to paradise. He had heard people describe this feeling of floating away in the first instance and assumed it would be about the same in death.

Wind rushed by his face snapping him out of his musings about what would happen if he died. He looked up and saw that Atherton carried him.

Nothing made sense to him at the moment. At least why they glided through the air made no sense. He thought Elyon stripped Atherton of his wings when the guardian ignored Elyon's orders and he helped Kenneth save his wife and child before.

Kenneth did not speak. He allowed the guardian to fly uninterrupted. The last thing that he wanted was for Atherton to become distracted and drop him. He watched the scenery below pass by at about the same speed as a strong horse at full gallop.

He had only flown one other time. About four years ago before Ethan was crowned king. The dragon Kyros took them in his claws and flew from just north of the lake to Mina's home. He did not like it then and did not like it now.

He watched the ground to see if they were being tracked. No soldiers or horses followed them. Silently Kenneth thanked Elyon for the rescue. It could have only been him who restored Atherton's wings.

He saw the path they flew along would take them behind the castle, over the forest and to the lake. From this height Kenneth saw figures on the shore of Lake Shiloh.

He could not tell who they were but could tell they were on horseback. Atherton adjusted his wings slightly and they began to glide toward the lake.

With several strong beats of his wings the guardian picked up speed. He folded them in tight and began a steady dive toward the figures lakeside. Kenneth felt his stomach jump into his throat.

The wind blew faster and his arms and legs flailed useless as they dove. Kenneth began to panic. He knew the guardian held him securely and he trusted Atherton completely. It was just the ground came at him so quickly. He tried to focus on something else.

At what seemed to be the last moment before the pair would crash, the guardian pulled straight up and slowly floated to the ground like a loose feather drifting on the wind.

The landing jarred Kenneth's knees slightly but he was safe. Once he was on the ground he saw the figures up close. The horseman he thought he saw from above turned out to be centaurs.

Several guardians and soldiers milled about. A soldier approached him and used the knife that Kenneth took from Roland to cut his hands free. Kenneth thanked the young man and retrieved the blade. He had future plans for the weapon.

Ulysses stood among the centaurs. His large friend walked to him. Kenneth extended his hand. The centaur nearly crushed it when he shook it.

"I am glad to see you," Kenneth said.

"It is good to see you both still have your heads," his centaur friend replied.

Krysta ran and collided with him, nearly knocking both of them to the ground. Her arms surrounded him and she kissed him hard. She nearly pulled him to the ground with the hold she had on him. He did not resist. He kissed her back and got lost in her touch. It thrilled him to see her again.

"How did you get here? Where's the baby?" Kenneth asked when she finally gave him a chance to speak.

"The prophet and Commander Amyx retrieved them," Ulysses said. "Had I set one hoof around the castle, I was sure to join the two of you."

Kenneth looked behind his friend. The dark haired young commander held Olin in his arms. His pale face, made him look weak and sickly. The commander had been stuck in bed since Ethan disappeared as he recovered from wounds he received while defending the king.

Kenneth approached the commander and gently took his son from the soldier. He cradled the boy in his arms and softly kissed his head. Joy rushed over him. His family was safe. The baby looked up at him with dark blue eyes and he smiled. Kenneth stroked the few strands of brownish red hair on the boy's head.

Anger took over as he thought about what this impostor had done to him. "Someone, please provide some answers for me?"

He looked at Atherton first who now wore a brilliant white cloak like he did before he was exiled. "Why do you have wings?"

"Elyon has restored me as a guardian for not believing and bowing down to this impostor," Atherton explained.

Kenneth handed the baby to Krysta. A female centaur intercepted the child. Kenneth began to protest but Ulysses' large hand on his shoulder stopped his words from being spoken.

"Krysta and the child will be taken to my village. No one there will bow to anyone but Elyon. Your family will be safe. Bivin will carry the child for Krysta while she rides. Her embrace is strong and gentle. He will be able to sleep the whole ride," Ulysses explained.

Kenneth eyed the female centaur. Her hair and horse body were both slightly less copper in color than Ulysses. Her face was very feminine and as fair as any woman Kenneth had ever seen.

Unlike Ulysses, Bivin wore a sleeveless shirt made of deerskin to cover her human torso. Though she was smaller than Ulysses, her arms were just as muscled. The sword she wore on her back was as large as the one Ulysses carried.

He hesitated and looked at Krysta. She smiled softly and nodded her agreement.

"Let us go with the centaurs," she said.

"I can't lose you two again," Kenneth replied. He did not know the reason for his hesitation.

"You won't. We trust Ulysses. He wouldn't put either of us in harm's way."

"I trusted Ethan too and almost lost my head for it," Kenneth said as he looked to his centaur friend.

"I understand, Kenneth," Ulysses replied. "Look into my eyes. You were able to see through the impostor."

He looked up at Ulysses. The centaur's face looked normal. The icy cold gaze and granite chiseled features stared back at him. In his heart Kenneth knew he could trust Ulysses but his head questioned if he could truly trust anyone anymore.

"Kenneth," Atherton interjected. "Search your heart. Let Elyon guide you to the truth."

Kenneth tried to allow his spirit to guide him. Elyon had been guiding him as of late. Peace, suddenly came upon him. All of his anger toward the impostor king dissipated as he held his son.

He knew he could trust Ulysses. He knew that Ethan had not betrayed him. He had been betrayed by the impostor. The man needed to be stopped.

He looked to Krysta again and gave a slight nod. "Alright. They go."

"They will be safe," the centaur repeated. He lifted his chin motioning to the other centaurs. Bivin secured the baby in a sling across the front of her body. A horse was brought for Krysta. She embraced her husband and kissed him long.

"I need you to come back to get us. Do what you have to in order to find the real Ethan and save the kingdom. Just come back to us." She kissed him hard one last time and then mounted the horse.

Kenneth watched her ride off with Commander Amyx, Bivin and about a dozen other centaurs. They rode north and then to the west along the lakeshore. Kenneth watched the group in silence until the last centaur could no longer be seen. He took a deep breath.

Elyon, keep them safe, he prayed silently.

"They will be kept safe," Ulysses said.

"I know," Kenneth said as he turned to his friends. "Who is this fake king?" he asked.

Ulysses shook his head. "I'm not sure," the centaur said. He motioned to the remaining centaur. "Before we get too detailed in discussions we should move. We can't risk being captured before we have a full understanding of what is really going on."

His centaur friend was right. The fake king practically went crazy searching for Vanacore and the other prisoner. He had to have had the entire army searching for Kenneth and Atherton by now. Soon they would be discovered if they waited any longer.

"Where do we go?" Atherton asked.

"Tilibra," Ulysses answered as he began walking away.

One last centaur led a pair of horses to Kenneth and Atherton. He handed the reins to the two of them. As soon as he relinquished the leather straps, he turned toward Ulysses.

They grasped each other's forearms in a traditional centaur greeting. The centaur Kenneth did not know offered a few words of encouragement and galloped off in the direction the others had gone. Ulysses started walking in the opposite direction. Kenneth and Atherton mounted their horses and rode after Ulysses.

Kenneth decided it was time to get answers. He caught up to Ulysses. "Tell me what you know," he said.

"Not much. The impostor is a sorcerer. His name is Alaric. That is all that I was able to learn so far."

"Just Alaric?" Kenneth asked.

"That was all my source knew," the centaur answered.

"So basically we know nothing," Kenneth said flatly. His patience grew thin. He needed some answers. Someone had to know something.

"I would not say that. I think we may have some allies to the north," Ulysses said.

"Who?" asked Atherton.

"Kiat. We may be able to catch him and help free his people," Ulysses explained.

"That's a start," Kenneth replied weakly.

The trio remained silent for a few moments as they moved forward. "There is one more thing. I also believe, and this is complete speculation on my part, but I believe that Ethan is alive," Ulysses said.

Kenneth was about to ask for clarification when the answer came to him. "The prisoner that escaped with Vanacore. That is why Alaric was so angry they got away."

Kenneth did not know why he did not see it sooner. You didn't see it because he's a sorcerer who wanted it hid from you.

"Precisely," Ulysses replied.

"Where are they now?" Atherton asked.

The centaur stopped and shrugged his massive shoulders. "North was all I could determine. My guess is they at least left Eden. If it were me, I would have gone into Tilibra.

"Then we ride for Tilibra," Kenneth said and spurred his horse forward.

chapter 14

Ethan did not understand why Elyon or the prophet had not told him where to find Trian Maras. He had returned to Midlothia, the last place he knew Trian to be, only to find the fortress abandoned.

The keep of this castle would have been the most secure place in the kingdom. Basically a spoiled coward, Trian would opt to be in the most secure area possible. At least that is what Ethan thought.

Currently they camped just outside a village not far from the walled fortress. Ethan sent Captain Casser and a couple of men to gather some further provisions and intelligence on the whereabouts of the play king of Tilibra.

Gerard gathered more than Ethan hoped he would. The captain returned with additional supplies, information and half dozen deserters from the army.

These men witnessed the battle between Ethan and the rider Famine. Trian had remained in the fortress like Ethan had suspected for several days. Then ordered for the army to march to the palace and leave Midlothia behind. These men had families in the village and stayed behind to try to protect them. They guessed Trian either did not know or care about their desertion. No one from the army returned.

When Gerard started asking about Trian, these men and others cornered him and forced him to explain why he wanted to know. Gerard stated he was with the King of Eden but that did not impress anyone. It was only when he referenced the victory over the Najera did these men let him return with answers. Six men joined the battle.

Ethan's small army now numbered about twenty. He stood at the perimeter of their campsite alone with his thoughts. The sun had just gone down and the sky had the grey twilight hue just before the blackness of night fully took over. He wondered if he would be able to get further answers from Trian. He needed to know the connection between Trian, Wakenda and Alaric Krollnoss.

Gerard joined him. "The night watch has been set. You should get some sleep."

Ethan turned to his captain. Shadows from the campfire behind them danced on the man's face.

'Sleep is something a king knows little of."

The king looked back at the horizon. At first he thought his tired mind played tricks on him. He thought he saw the darkness move.

"To arms!" Gerard shouted as he drew his sword.

Ethan then saw the movement clearly. Three horses trotted to them. Or more precisely two horses and a centaur. The stranger's faces came into view. Faces that Ethan was all too glad to see.

"Hold!" Ethan commanded raising an arm to the men behind him. "These are friends."

Ethan approached the centaur and offered his hand. The centaur did not respond right away. His suspicions had help keep Ethan alive over the last several years.

Mina ran out to Ethan's side. The eyes of the riders grew wide at the sight of her. Kenneth drew his sword. Ethan raised his hands and stood between them. He always sensed what his friend thought but his intentions were clear this time. He remembered Mina's betrayal all too well.

"No wait," Ethan said.

"Who are you?" Kenneth asked.

"You may have known me as Benniah Deweago but my name is Ethan Lyons."

The three of them looked suspiciously at Ethan. He turned to Gerard and tilted his head toward the fire. Gerard retreated to the fire and returned holding a torch. The flame danced around but allowed his friends to see his face. They still did not seem convinced.

Ethan looked at Kenneth. "You have a scar on the bridge of your nose. The result of a cut caused by a small shield I threw at you when we were about ten years old."

Kenneth showed off his crooked teeth when he smiled widely. Born a couple of years before Ethan, Kenneth had been his friend for a long time. He stood only slightly taller than Ethan with thick black hair and dark brown eyes. He dismounted and ran to the king. He embraced his friend and held Ethan probably a little longer than he should have.

When Kenneth released Ethan, the king stuck his hand out to the centaur. This time his captain of the guard clasped Ethan's forearm and smiled. Ulysses did not smile often but it was good to see that his usually stone cold face could still do that. The third man dismounted his horse. Gerard walked to him and took the horse's leads from him.

Dressed in brilliant white, Atherton approached the king. They also clasped forearms. Gerard returned to the reunited group of friends after delegating the care of the horses and releasing the men. Ethan made introductions all around.

"Let's go sit by the fire and talk," Mina suggested.

"First, why is she here?" Kenneth asked. His mood jumped from joyous to suspicious. "She tried to kill you, or don't you remember?"

"I remember."

Gerard excused himself from the conversation to return to his men.

"That does not answer why she is here?"

"She's your sister, Kenneth," Ethan said trying to reason with his friend. "Besides she helped me escape Krollnoss' death sentence."

It took Kenneth a moment to understand the implications of what Ethan said. His eyes widened with anger when he realized what Ethan meant.

"You are Vanacore."

"I *was* Vanacore," she replied.

Kenneth stepped toward her. Ethan realized his intentions were not good. "I have forgiven her for what happened when *your* father tried to steal my kingdom."

Kenneth ignored Ethan's words or did not hear them at all in his state of anger. Ethan stepped between them. Kenneth looked at him for the first time since he realized who Mina had been hiding as.

"Did you know what that man did to my family? Did you know what he did to my son?" Kenneth's voice grew louder. Atherton and Ulysses each gripped one of his shoulders in an attempt to restrain him.

"I am sorry about your son's death, Kenneth. I truly am," she said.

Ethan realized the noise he woke up to that morning in the dungeon was Krysta mourning their child. He stepped forward and hugged Kenneth.

"I am so sorry, my friend."

Ethan's gesture took Kenneth out of his anger. "No, my son is alive, now."

The king released his friend. "I guess now is the time we catch everybody up. Starting with if your son is alive why are you now angry at Mina?"

When Kenneth did not speak Atherton interjected. "The sorcerer has convinced everyone he is you. He does look more like you than you do."

"That's another long story that we will fill you in on soon enough. Tell me what is going on in Eden. What happened to your son?"

Kenneth looked at Ethan. "The fake you has claimed that Elyon has appointed him or you as His prophet. To prove it, he set up a demonstration of miracles. One of which was he raised Olin from the dead."

"He raised your father from the dead?" Ethan asked confused.

"No, Olin is what we decided to name our son. Olin Vaughn Tudyck."

Mina reached her arms out to embrace her brother. Kenneth stopped her before she got around Ethan.

"Did you know that he kidnapped our son, replaced him with another dead child and let us believe for a week that our son was dead? You and that despicable Roland were supposed to be his closest advisors."

"No, Kenneth. I swear I did not know that. Krollnoss did not explain his plans to me to the same extent as he did Roland. I suppose he did not trust me as much as I thought he did."

Kenneth considered her answer and seemed satisfied. They retreated to the warmth of the fire. Ulysses and Kenneth ate while they everyone talked.

Kenneth, Ulysses and Atherton took turns telling them about what had happened since Ethan disappeared. They shared about how Krysta was kidnapped by Charax the demon so that he could be a sacrifice offered by the followers of some other demon who claimed to be a god and would return someday.

Kenneth explained his suspicions about the sorcerer, Roland and Vanacore. Atherton explained how he disobeyed other directives from Elyon while he remained in Eden to help find Ethan and rescue Krysta and the baby. Kenneth shared how he turned his life over to Elyon and how he learned to trust Kiat and the Tulchin elves.

In turn Mina shared what happened to her after their father's failed attempt at stealing the kingdom from Ethan. She shared what she knew of Alaric's plan including why the sorcerer looked like Ethan.

The king filled the others in on his adventure. How he washed up on the shore of Rathua, was befriended by Meldorn and how he and Captain Casser met. He told the others about Trian and how he recruited the king to kill a dragon that released the Najera.

It was late into the night when everyone finished their stories.

"Krollnoss cast the spell to take my memory and likeness away so he could replace me as king. He then proclaim's that he is Elyon's messenger here."

"To what ends though?" Kenneth asked.

"Domination," Ethan said after a moment of thought. "He has already taken two kingdom's. One by force and one by deception. He must be set on taking over the world."

Ulysses asked, "You keep calling him Krollnoss. As in Xestes Krollnoss?"

Mina and Ethan looked at each other. "Alaric is the older brother of Xestes."

Each of his friends took the news in their own way but all seemed just as surprised as Ethan was when he found out. They broke up the meeting for sleep. Atherton took up watch with the other guards. They would march to Trian's palace in the morning and remove him from power.

chapter 15

Elyon spoke to Ethan through a number of ways. Sometimes the wild-haired prophet would show up with a message. Many times Ethan "heard" Elyon's voice speak to his spirit. He could never really explain what he experienced in these times. The best explanation he could give Kenneth when he asked was it was like a thought that came to him from out of nowhere. He just knew that the message was from Elyon.

Two nights prior Elyon spoke to the king while he slept. Familiar nightmares haunted Ethan that night. His nightmares had not come for him in the dark since well before Krollnoss had stolen his memory. When he awoke the next morning he recalled the details of an odd dream sandwhiched between the nightmares.

Amber Maras sat in the corner of a small wooden shack crying. Ethan sensed she was afraid. He called out to her but she did not answer. She looked up at him but did not seem to see him. Her cheeks were red and glistened from all the tears that flowed down her face. Ethan reached out to her. He ran to her holding out his hands. The harder he ran the further away she seemed to be.

Ethan stopped running and again Amber seemed to be just within arms reach. The shack they were in had no furniture aside from the chair she sat on and a small table. He walked to the door and turned the handle. It was locked. He tried to open the two small windows. They would not budge. He punched the glass in the windows. Nothing happened.

In the blink of an eye he found himself engulfed in darkness. The king saw people wearing rags. Many people worked at breaking rocks off of the wall of the cave. Others pushed carts full of rocks. Were they carving the cave? No, they were mining. He woke knowing they would find Trian at his slave encampment in the western mountains. Elyon had showed him that was where the tyrant would be.

Gerard and the other men of Tilibra questioned Ethan's sanity when he shared this new plan with them. Mina even argued against going to the mines. As Vanacore she had some contact with the spoiled tyrant and insisted he would not be at the mines. He hated the outdoors.

Ethan assured his leaders Elyon had shown him where to find the evil king. Ulysses, Kenneth and Atherton supported Ethan's explanation. They were willing to pack up and head west. In the end, Ethan used his title to get the men moving in the direction he wanted.

"I am king," he had said. "Anyone can leave at anytime. If you remain, be packed and ready to move." No one else disputed his word.

After two days of travel the small army set up camp within sight of the foothills of the mountains where Trian kept his slaves working day and night. Gerard confirmed the wagon trail that started at the base of the mountain. That night Gerard, Kenneth and Ethan rode closer to the mountain but not so close that a passing patrol would spot them.

"There is the main entrance," Gerard explained. "Trian has wagons that go up every couple of days. The road inclines gradually until it reaches the plateau where most of the digging is done."

Ethan stood silently trying to form a plan that would be as safe as possible for the slaves and cause the fewest causalities on both sides. He did not see a way to accomplish both.

"There are no other paths up the mountain?"

"There is a game trail to the east of here," Gerard said. "More like a goat trail. It is steep and can be climbed by humans, but is too narrow for horses, so Ulysses won't be able to go with us."

Ethan thought a moment. "Surprise is going to be our best ally. I want as few casualties as possible."

"If we capture Trian and the Rathuan quickly, the men should surrender," Kenneth said.

"Do you think you would be able to talk the soldiers into surrendering?" the king asked Gerard.

"Possibly, but I don't think Goemaere Wakenda is going to give up very easily," Gerard replied.

Ethan folded his arms and stood silent for several moments. "Mina will wait with Ulysses at the foot of the mountain."

Another moment of silence passed. Kenneth spoke, "She's not going to like that."

"I know but it will be for her own safety."

Kenneth faced his friend. "Her safety or your peace of mind?"

"A bit of both," Ethan answered.

chapter 16

The sun had been up for a couple of hours when Ethan and his men began the trek up the mountain. He led his few men along the narrow path. Mina and Ulysses remained at the bottom.

The king found it a blessing and a curse that the centaur could not climb the path. He felt it was a curse due to missing the mighty Ulysses in a potential battle. With only a dozen men with him Elyon would surely have to provide the victory if they were to free the slaves.

Though he would miss Ulysses in battle, Ethan felt blessed to have the centaur wait with Mina away from the danger. He knew she could take care of herself.

He witnessed her skills firsthand but if she were in the fight then he would not be able to focus on the mission. It was good she remained with Ulysses, however unwillingly on her part. Kenneth was right. Mina did not like his decision to leave her with the centaur but she accepted it.

They reached a ridge that overlooked the main mining camp. Below Ethan saw soldiers moving in and out of dozens of canvas shelters. Anger flared inside him as a woman was dragged by two soldiers into one of those tents. Her ragged clothes barely covering her body. She screamed and fought against her captors but they only laughed, picked her up and took her inside.

Trian sat on a high backed ornate chair. He looked like a spoiled child who could be disturbed with nothing except if it affected his toys. This false king did not even bother turn at the woman's cries. The King of Eden drew his sword. He heard the ring of the other swords being unsheathed as his men followed his lead.

Movement caught Ethan's eye. The black centaur strode confidently to Trian. His soldiers forced the slaves who were outside the mine back into the mouth of the cavern. Ethan stopped a moment. He wanted to know what was happening. His eyes darted between Trian and the centaur and the soldiers pushing the slaves around.

Trian's soldiers began pushing the centaur's men. A large elf leaped from the crowd at the mouth of the mine and climbed the face of the mountain like a spider crawling up a wall. Ethan's mind began to work. The spider like elf reached the top. He pulled a large battle ax off of his back and began to take aim. He positioned himself to slam the axe into the rock.

"They're going to bury those people in the mine," he said. "Take that elf down!" Ethan stood.

He climbed over the the ridge and slid down the more gentle slope. Attention was momentarily drawn to him. The closest resistance came from Trian's men.

Ethan easily blocked a strike from a young man, more like a teenage kid who was undoubtedly pressed into the service of this false king. Ethan knocked the young man's sword to the ground and finished with a left hook to his jaw. The man fell with a thud.

Ethan continued on to his target. One of the men who had dragged the woman into the tent approached him. Ethan wasted no time trading blows with him, with one swing of his sword he slashed the other's throat.

The second soldier exited the tent buckling his sword belt as he did. Ethan stopped long enough to pull a knife out of the belt of the man's fallen partner and threw it. The blade embedded into the man's chest.

Ethan glanced at the elf above the entrance to the mine. Two arrows stuck in each of his shoulders but he still slammed the large ax blade into the ground.

Rocks began to fall. Ethan yelled his command for someone to stop the elf again. Another arrow flew across the gap, this time striking the handle of the battle ax.

A flash of light momentarily filled the skies. The elf crashed the ax to the ground again. The struggles in the camp ceased while everyone watched as Atherton flew across to the other ridge.

Ethan tore his eyes from the sight of the guardian and took advantage of the situation. He put down two more men and an elf. He was beginning to have a hard time determining which man was with which army.

He saw a standing Trian shout orders to the men. Geomare Wakenda ignored the boy king's orders. He locked his gaze on Ethan. Wakenda stepped off of the dais and took a few steps toward Ethan with a sword drawn.

"Don't just stand there, do something!" Trian screamed at the dark centaur.

With speed Ethan had only seen matched by Ulysses the black centaur drew an arrow and fired it into Trian's throat. The creature turned like he simply ended a conversation and walked back down the main path. He paid no further attention to the chaos around him.

Wakenda never looked back. He kept his eyes trained on Ethan. He was bent on revenge.

All around him, Ethan saw the slaves fighting back and the elves and men who came with the centaur retreating. He and the fat Rathuan stopped a short distance from each other.

"I am going to finish you this time boy," he growled. "I see the old man is not here to help you. Did he finally die?"

Again Ethan's anger boiled to the top. He had not known Meldorn for a long time but they were friends and he was not going to stand for such disrespect.

"Prepare to join him, Benniah Deweago."

"My name is not Benniah. I am Ethan Lyons, King of Eden and Warrior of Elyon. Trian is dead." Ethan pointed at the body on the ground behind Wakenda.

"Your conqueror is no more. Help me free your people from an evil sorcerer."

"I must have hit you harder than I thought in our last fight. That boy could not conquer a field full of sheep. I will kill you then I will join the true king who by now has become a god," Wakenda chuckled. He walked toward Ethan. His intention to fight was clear.

Ethan blocked the swings of the man's sword with his own. The metal clanged as they exchanged blows. Wakenda drew a dagger from his belt. Ethan answered with the hunting knife from his boot.

Again the blades clanged as each blow was struck and blocked. Neither man could gain the advantage over the other. Finally Wakenda kicked Ethan in the knee. The king stumbled. It gave the other the time pull his sword up high and slice downward. The strike clanked on Ethan's sword again but this time his weapon fell from his hand.

Ethan responded with an upward strike of his own with his hunting knife. The blade of his knife cut the forearm of Wakenda's dagger hand.

The fat man jerked his hand back and released the dagger. Ethan sprang back up to two feet. The Rathuan quickly regained his composure. He thrust his sword at Ethan's belly.

The king sidestepped the attack. He wrapped his arm over and around his opponent's. Goemaere struggled but could not free himself. Ethan turned at his waist and slammed his free elbow into the nose of the other. He heard and felt the crunch as it broke and felt the warm blood spill onto his arm.

Wakenda dropped the sword. Ethan released him and allowed him to stumble back. The king turned to face his enemy again. "You can end this anytime by surrendering. I do not want to hurt you."

The answer came in the form of a beastly roar. With his nose mangled and blood pouring down his mouth, Wakenda appeared more monster than man. Ethan realized the man likely still blamed him for the death of his son. The Rathuan roared again and charged the king.

Ethan was not able to dodge the man this time. Wakenda grabbed Ethan's throat as he fell on the king. Ethan felt the breath leave him. With the massive man laying on him he could not regain his breath easily.

The zip of an arrow flying through the air took his attention off of his enemy for a moment. Wakenda stiffened, released his grip and rolled off of the king. He roared again.

Ethan coughed and tried to suck in air at the same time. He finally got breath back into his body and stood. Goemaere also stood. An arrow protruded from the back of his shoulder.

Anger blinded the man to his physical pain. He reached out and grabbed Ethan by his vest and pulled him off of his feet. Ethan felt like a child being lifted by his father, albeit a very angry father.

He tried to kick the other but his feet only bounced off of the man's gut. He punched Wakenda in the face two and then three times. The fourth time the man dropped him and staggered back a few steps.

When he landed, his hands felt something metal. The hilt of the Rathuan's dagger lay at his hand. He wrapped his fingers around the weapon.

"Surrender, Wakenda. Your leader is dead," Ethan said.

"I never followed that spineless boy. Krollnoss will reward me when I kill you."

Goemaere charged again. Ethan lifted the weapon. The blade pushed into the top of the man's belly right below his chest. The dagger sunk to the hilt.

Ethan stood. Wakenda dropped to his knees and then onto his side. He released one last gasp of breath. All other fighting ceased. Trian was dead. His lieutenant also dead. All eyes looked to the King of Eden.

He surveyed the battlefield. A few soldiers and slaves lay dead. Only Atherton stood above the mouth of the mine. Those who were forced into it now gathered around. Kenneth looked alright.

"People of Tilibra, you are free. King Vincent Maras is free and is again your rightful king." He paused more to catch his breath than for any other reason. "People of Rathua, Goemaere Wakenda is dead. I know what has become of your home. You are also free."

One of the men in a tattered Rathuan garment stepped forward. "What do you know of us? You washed up on our shores only a few weeks ago."

"True. I lived with Meldorn among your people for only a few weeks but I know of your troubles."

Another Rathuan spoke up, "Who are you anyway?"

"I am Ethan Lyons, King of Eden."

Many of the slaves instinctively dropped to one knee in respect at the mention of a king being among them.

"Are we to be grateful to you and pledge our allegiance to you because you killed our leader?" The first man asked. "You can enslave us just as easily."

Ethan did not understand this reaction. It made no sense to him. Wakenda essentially traded them for his own freedom and they were treated lower than the dirt they stood on yet they seemed to hate him.

"No, I do not wish to enslave you. I want to ask for your help to free my kingdom from an impostor and to offer you refuge."

"I, for one, will not be fodder for your army," the man replied. He turned his back and many of the others followed him.

Three women pushed their way through the crowd. One ran to Gerard. She wrapped her arms around him and kissed him. Tears poured down her face. She no doubt was his wife. The second woman was Amber Maras, who ran to Ethan and nearly knocked him over. She kissed Ethan long and hard.

Ethan heard Kenneth clear his throat. He gently pushed Amber to arms length. He saw Mina standing in front of him and flashed an innocent grin her way. Mina's arms crossed over her chest. Her glare pierced him deeper than the dagger that went into Wakenda.

"Mina, I can explain. This is Amber Maras, Princess of Tilibra. She was just expressing her thanks for saving her people."

Amber looked from Ethan to Mina. "Benniah, I don't understand. I thought we had a connection," the princess said.

Ethan wished Elyon would cause a whirlwind to take him away. "Um—," The words would not come to him. Mina had no such trouble.

"Well, *princess*, first he is not Benniah, this is Ethan Lyons, King of Eden. He does not have a connection with you…" She was clearly jealous.

Ethan was happy that Ulysses changed the subject. "We saw Beserth and his men ride off quickly. I thought we should ride up the mountain on the main wagon road to see if you needed any help."

Ethan glanced at Mina. She focused her angry glare back and forth between he and Amber. He opened his mouth to speak when Kenneth spoke.

"Ethan, I want you to meet Tennia Fambre, wife of Kiat." A bronzed female elf stood next to his friend. She bowed her head in respect.

"It is a pleasure to finally meet you. Kiat has spoken highly of you," Ethan said.

She bowed at the waist. "The honor is mine. Kiat had often spoken of your nobility while he was home. I can say that his description of your honor goes well with your bravery."

"Thank you. I am humbled by your words," Ethan replied.

"What do we do now?" Mina asked. Her tone reflected her anger.

Gerard and his wife concluded their reunion and the captain now joined the circle. "We should go to King Vincent. He is indebted to you. You saved his life, his daughter and his kingdom. He is sure to help you in your quest to overcome your enemy."

Tennia spoke. "We are indebted to you as well. We can spare about fifty warriors. I need the rest to guide the women and children back to Quantas."

Ethan gave a single nod in response to the offer. "Your help will be appreciated." He looked at Gerard. "Let's go see the king."

chapter 17

Three days after the battle at the mines, Ethan found himself again at the palace in Tilibra. This time in the presence of the real king of Tilibra. This time Ethan was introduced as King of Eden instead of a man without a kingdom.

Vincent Maras decided he would not leave it to a foreign stranger to return his throne to him and began marshaling forces on his way back to the palace. Upon learning this news Kenneth remarked he could have decided that earlier and things may have been a little different. Ethan reminded his friend to not speak like that as they were under King Maras' hospitality.

Ethan and his friends were given comfortable rooms, clean clothes and an opportunity to become presentable again before entering the presence of the king. Ethan appreciated the gesture but was anxious to get back to Eden. He needed a quick answer from the king of Tilibra and would be on his way no matter the outcome. Finally a thin servant called for Ethan. Mina, Kenneth and Gerard went into the presence of King Maras with him.

The king sat in his throne on the dais where not long ago, Trian sat when Ethan and Meldorn were first brought to the palace. Queen Maras sat on the king's right and Amber on his left. Ethan glanced over his shoulder at Mina. She glared at the princess. He was glad to see that Mina still cared so deeply for him but thought she may have been overreacting just a little.

The visitors knelt after being escorted to the throne room. The king stood. "Rise, my friends. You have no need to kneel before me. I should kneel before you."

He motioned for a soldier to step forward. The man carried a black bow and quiver.

"These, I believe, belong to you," King Maras said. The soldier presented the weapon to Ethan.

The bow they had left with the archers at Gerard's safe house. They would need this for the next half of their journey. Ethan bowed his head while accepting the items.

"Thank you, majesty. These will be put to good use in the battle to come."

"It is I who ought to thank you, King Ethan. You have saved my life, my family and my kingdom. If you would indulge me a moment. What news do you have of Jonathan Prador? I thought he was your ally but I do not see him with you."

Ethan looked at Gerard. "Prador is a traitor. He betrayed us and took the other weapons and the medallion. He murdered my friend and nearly killed the captain."

"I knew he could not be trusted."

"And something in my spirit told *me* not to trust him but foolishly, I didn't listen."

Ethan handed the bow and quiver to Gerard as a gesture that he intended to change the subject. The captain accepted both and slung them over his shoulder.

"King Maras, I have come to you to ask for your help with saving my kingdom. A sorcerer by the name of Alaric Krollnoss has deceived my people. I humbly request your help in regaining my throne."

King Vincent paced the dais and looked at his wife and his daughter. "I have been exiled from my own throne for a number of years. I cannot assist you in your quest."

"I have reason to believe that your son, Trian, may have been working with this sorcerer. I believe the sorcerer helped Trian usurp your throne," Ethan said hoping to bolster his case.

"I am sorry." King Maras looked to the left like he was ashamed of his son. He did not speak another word but sat back down on his throne.

Ethan thought a moment. He searched for any truth that may convince the king to help. "If I am defeated, it will only be a matter of time before the sorcerer sets his sight back on Tilibra."

"Then I pray you are victorious but I cannot help you beyond providing you and those who ride with you horses, weapons and provisions for the journey."

Gerard suddenly spoke. "Food and weapons? Horses? Is that how you repay the debt that you owe this man? Not only did King Lyons save your life and your family but he saved your kingdom. You said so yourself."

"I will be eternally grateful for what he has done but I cannot participate in battles that are not mine, especially with an army as fragmented as mine. After all, captain, if memory serves me, you served my treacherous son until only recently."

"That is true but the man standing before you also saved my entire world. For that I will do what you are unwilling to do." Gerard dropped to one knee. "I swear my life and my sword to your service, King Lyons."

King Maras was visibly upset. Gerard had insulted him in his own home. Ethan knew he would have to say something quickly but before he could think of anything Gerard spoke again.

"I am no coward and will do what is necessary."

"That is enough!" King Maras stood. "How dare you speak to me like that. I *am* the king of Tilibra and these are my halls. You may have just sworn your allegiance to another but I could still have you executed," said King Vincent.

Ethan raised a hand and stepped forward.

"Please, majesty, spare his life. He may have spoke out of line but if I am to succeed then I will need every man I can muster. I appreciate the assistance that you can provide."

Ethan's diplomacy seemed to defuse the matter. King Maras sat back on his throne. Ethan motioned for Gerard to stand. The captain did so.

"We will take our leave as soon as the provisions you have promised are assembled."

Ethan bowed his head and he and his friends returned to his chambers to discuss their journey further. After they planned their route South, Kenneth, Ulysses and Tennia left to make sure the men would be ready the moment the provisions were.

Ethan sent Gerard on ahead of them in order to settle his wife into one of his safe houses. Captain Casser's absence, he hoped would settle King Vincent further.

"Princess or not, I still don't like that that girl kissed you," Mina said when they were alone. "Did you see the way she looked at you?"

"You have no need to worry, my love," Ethan replied. He gave her a quick kiss and her mood lightened. "Will you go and help the others? I want to pray alone."

She nodded and smiled. Ethan loved her smile. He always had. Her smile is what he first noticed about her. Most men noticed some of her other features but he saw her smile first. She kissed him and turned to do as he had asked her.

When she had closed the door to the bed chamber he had been assigned by King Maras, he got down on his knees. The stone floor hurt them but he ignored the pain. He began to worship Elyon.

"Elyon, you alone have brought me this far. You are *the* God of gods. There is no other like you. You are perfect in your mercy and your wisdom. Guide me."

He sat there whispering praise to Elyon. Finally he bent over and placed his forehead to the stone floor in worship. Then he heard it. A voice he had heard many times over the last few years. Quiet and gentle yet full of authority. It spoke to his spirit.

"Trust me. I am your army. I will fight your battle."

chapter 18

Alaric grew tired of waiting for his men to find the fugitives. No one had found Vanacore and Lyons. Ulysses vanished and now Atherton and Tudyck escaped execution. He could not allow them to escape. They had to be caught. They had to die otherwise his word was worth nothing. Roland and Beserth and the entire army of Eden could not locate these four men and one centaur.

He hated doing things himself but he decided to make the exception for them. When he found them they would all die slowly and painfully. Roland searched in the West. Beserth should return from Tilibra any day now.

Alaric and Jonathan searched the villages to the North. They had yet to find a sign of any of them. The only good Alaric had seen from this search was that more and more people were worshipping him just as planned. Village after village had surrendered and bowed to him with a minimal number of executions.

The sorcerer rode high in the saddle as they entered yet another village he did not bother to learn the name of. His guards forced the people to the square. Men, women and children all gathered to hear him speak. They gathered willingly or were dragged out of their homes. He noticed many in this village were elderly or young children. He shrugged. It made no difference to him their ages. Just as long as they bowed to him.

"I am Ethan Lyons, King of Eden, and Elyon in the flesh. I am looking for a few men and a centaur. Fugitives. They are dangerous. Have there been any who do not belong who have come through here recently?" he said.

Again he hated introducing himself as Lyons. He had to for now. In the coming months, when all have either bowed or died. He will reveal his true name. He would tell the world that Elyon has decreed he change his name and it would be so. The world would then truly worship Alaric Krollnoss.

An old man carrying a leather book that appeared as old as he was stood and stepped forward. "I know who you really are. Elyon told me."

"Good. Then you know to answer my question. Have any strange men ridden through here?"

"I am not afraid of you."

The man now began to bother Alaric. "You really should be, especially if you know who I am. You should also know what I am capable of. I am a god in the flesh. I can destroy you for eternity."

The old man smiled. "I am the priest of Elyon in this village. He told me you would come. He also gave me a message for you."

The man's comment intrigued the sorcerer. Alaric decided not to kill him just yet. "Really? What is the message you have for me?"

"The destroyer will find you. Run where you may but you will be found out. You will be exposed and the real Elyon will be praised far and wide. He who can see, let him see this man is not who he says he is. He who can hear, let him here the word of the living Elyon."

Alaric conjured a fireball. The green sphere floated over his open palm. The crowd gasped. With a thrust of his hands the flame shot toward the priest and struck him in the chest. The man wailed and screamed in agony as the fire spread first over his robes and then melted his skin. His cries lasted only a minute or two and then ceased.

Women began to cry at the sight. Children screamed and clung to their mothers in terror.

Alaric looked at those gathered. He changed the tone of his voice to one a commander would use to address his troops. He intended to put fear into these people so that no one else would stand up to him.

"I *am* Elyon in the flesh. He who doubts me will end up like this man." The sorcerer pointed at the scorched bones of the priest.

The cries of the women and children stopped. All was silent. The wind did not blow. The birds did not chirp. Not a sound could be heard in the village.

"Worship me or be put to death."

One after the other, the people knelt to the ground and bowed. They put their foreheads in the dirt and shouted praises to Elyon. Alaric smiled. He closed his eyes and held his arms out straight. He received the worship that the people put out. Songs began to be sung.

I could get used to this, he thought.

The sorcerer took a deep breath in but suddenly could not exhale. He could not move. He could not open his eyes. An unseen force held him in place. For the first time he reconsidered his plan of claiming to be Elyon.

Slowly an image formed in front of him. Three cloaked and hooded riders. One sat on a black horse. One rode a red horse. The one that concerned him the most sat atop a large pale horse. The animal was as large as Beserth. With eyes as red as blood it appeared to breathe fire out of its nose.

Around the riders appeared an army whose numbers had to be in the tens of thousands. He was certain the number of this army had never been seen before. He was also certain the purpose of this army was to lay waste to every living being in the world.

Men of every race stood in the army's ranks. Centaurs, manticores, griffins and magical beasts of every kind either served as a soldier's mount or stood next to the men. Behind the men stood orcs and goblins, riding their hideous mounts. A horde of armored skeletons armed with swords and axes made up the final line of the army. A pair of skeletal dragons suddenly emerged from behind them.

He smelled the smoke and sulfur from their fiery breath as they sent bursts of flames in his direction. He had never experienced a fear this great before. He tried to duck and roll out of the path of the inferno coming toward him but still could not move. The flames dispersed before reaching him.

The rider on the black horse shrieked a shrill cry that no human could ever mimic. He thought he felt his spine crawl out of his body at the sound. The rider on the red horse produced a flail that he swung overhead. The chain extended slightly with every turn until the spiked ball narrowly missed the sorcerer's nose but the sorcerer was powerless to move or stop the weapon.

The rider on the pale horse urged his mount forward a few steps. It raised a skeletal hand and pointed at Alaric. Then it dropped the hood of its cloak, exposing a red eyed skull. The creature cackled uncontrollably then raised a scythe. The blade of the tool came for the sorcerer's head.

The trance or spell released him. Alaric ducked and opened his eyes. The cackling laughter still in his ears faded away replaced by the songs to Elyon. The people still worshipped. He realized in that moment, they worshipped the real Elyon and not him.

A slight breeze kicked up. The robes of the dead priest flapped. Alaric saw the book the man held. He picked it up out of the man's ashes. The leather cover was tattered but the book had not burned. On the cover was the mark of a winged man. Alaric opened it to the first page. It read: *The Book of Elyon.*

He tossed it to the ground. The book opened randomly. The sentence at the top of the page read: *"No weapon formed can stand against those who stand with me."*

Alaric stood and sneered. Beserth stood in front of him. "What news do you have for me?"

The centaur looked down at him. Trian Maras has been eliminated. His father is retaking the throne."

Alaric waved his hand. "Vincent Maras is of not threat to us. Especially when I control the army of the Najera."

"Lyons was there."

"So that is where he is hiding."

"Tudyck, the guardian and Ulysses were also with him," the centaur reported.

"And Vanacore?"

Beserth shook his head. "No sign of him, sire."

"Then we move North," Alaric commanded.

"What of the village, brother?" Prador asked.

The sorcerer kicked the book and turned to his brother.

"Burn it. Burn everything. Every building, every crop and fruit tree. Burn it all to the ground and kill anyone who opposes you."

The worship stopped suddenly when the people heard his command. The cries of protest and fear filled the air as he mounted his horse and turned to Tilibra. It was a sound he had grown to like.

Jonathan rode up next to Alaric. "Brother, why do we ride to Tilibra?"

Alaric sensed a nervousness in his brother's voice. "Are you afraid to return?" the sorcerer sneered at his brother.

"No. I just do not see the wisdom in riding straight at the enemy. We should return to the castle where we have a position of strength. Lyons is sure to return to us."

"How do you know?"

"I don't but he seems to have an inner drive that does not let him just run. He barely knew Amber Maras but would not just leave her to the mercy of Trian."

Alaric thought about his brother's point. If the stories he had heard about Lyons and his honor were true, then he would return just as his brother said. Alaric had enough of riding anyway.

"You are right. That was a very good observation, Jonathan."

Alaric gave the order to return to Castle Bekah. He began riding South. The cry of the black rider in his vision rang in his ears again. He would have preferred the cackle of the skeleton rider. He sensed someone to his right.

"Brother, why won't you track the Najera?" Jonathan asked. "We have the weapons to destroy them. You can control their armies if we do that."

"I don't have anyone to fight them."

"I can do fight them. I have been training for years."

Alaric sighed. "I know but fighting the Najera is different than sparring with knights."

Jonathan rode silently for a moment. "You wish Xestes were here instead of me, don't you."

Of course I do.

Alaric sighed again. "I do wish he were here but not instead of you. The three of us should be ruling all kingdoms. To answer your next question, yes, if Xestes were here and he wanted to face the riders, I would allow him to."

"Why?"

"Because Xestes sharpened his skills on the battlefield. He would less likely be killed in the battle."

Jonathan dropped his head and fell in line with the troops.

Perhaps I should not have been so hard on him, Alaric thought

Alaric spurred his horse forward. He was finished with this talk. He would let the King of Eden battle the Najera. Suddenly he pulled up on his horse and turned the animal around. He looked his brother in the eyes.

"Lyons is expendable. I will let him and the Najera destroy each other. Then I alone will remain to rule. I will have no more talk about you fighting the Najera."

Alaric turned his horse again. All of their horses became hard to control as a shrill cry pierced the air. Alaric recognized the sound. He knew the riders were close. He was ready to be back home at Castle Bekah.

chapter 19

The provisions that King Maras promised took longer than Ethan would have liked to be assembled. Ethan and his small army left early the morning after Maras decided he would not provide troops to support the King of Eden. Gerard questioned why Ethan was not angrier than he had shown.

"Anger would only frustrate the situation more," the king had told his new Captain.

Ethan forced his army to ride through the day and the following night. His goal was to reach a small village he knew of a few miles south of the border with Tilibra. Just as the sun began its drop below the horizon the village came into sight.

They would stop there and stay with the people. These were good people that worshipped Elyon. They had helped him before he was king, when he was running from Xestes Krollnoss after his father was assassinated.

They will help us now too.

The riders rode into the heart of the village. Ethan barely stopped his horse before dismounting. He walked among the burnt out buildings. This small village was home to a community of about two hundred people. There was no sign of any of the villagers. Only a lonely wind blew over them.

"Lord Tudyck," a familiar voice called out. The group turned. Several swords rang as they were unsheathed. Ethan signaled for the swords to be put away as he recognized one of the bronze forms that approached him. Kiat Fambre and another Tulchin elf who stood a little taller than Atherton jogged toward them.

"Kiat, it is good to see you again," Kenneth said. He ran to meet the elf. He extended his hand and the two clasped the others forearm in greeting.

Ethan stood apparently alone in his confusion of what had just happened. Before Roland had abducted him on the beach in Myrtle, Kenneth had been spouting the reasons Kiat could not be trusted. Now they acted as if they were long lost friends seeing each other for the first time in years.

"Wait, I need someone to explain this," the king said pointing to the pair of smiling friends.

"It is a long story but suffice it to say that Kiat earned my trust," Kenneth answered as he released the other's arm.

"Lord Tudyck—,"

Kenneth put a hand in the air to cut the elf off. "I told you, my friends call me Kenneth."

Kiat nodded. "Old habits, my friend. Who is this man?"

Kenneth's smile turned from warm to mischievous. "You will not believe it."

Kiat put out his hands and said, "Try me."

Mina stepped forward. "This is Ethan Lyons, King of Eden," she said proudly.

The elf shook his head. "You are right I don't believe you. He was here a day and a half ago."

"Did he do this?" Ethan asked.

The elf's countenance fell, like he was ashamed of something.

"Yes, he killed the priest when he refused to bow down to him. Then he ordered the entire village to be razed. That is not like him, Kenneth. What is going on?"

"How do you know it was him?" Ethan asked.

"We saw him." The elf pointed to a field of what appeared to have been corn growing. "We were hiding in that field."

"It is not like him because it is not him," Kenneth said. "The Ethan you saw was a sorcerer called Alaric Krollnoss. He abducted Ethan and put a spell on him to remove his memory and apparently his likeness. His memory has returned but we have yet to figure out why he still does not look like himself."

"Then forgive me, majesty, for any disrespect I may have shown you," Kiat said bowing at the waist.

"It is not necessary. I am living it and still hardly believe. Where is Krollnoss now?"

"They returned to Castle Bekah," the tall elf growled more than spoke.

"How do you know?" Kenneth asked.

"A smaller man with dark hair spoke to Ethan and convinced him to go," the elf answered.

Kiat tapped his forehead, "Where are my manners? This is my brother Hennisus."

"It is my pleasure to meet you," Ethan said.

Tennia ran from the remaining troops. She jumped into Kiat's arms much like Mina used to do when she saw Ethan for the first time in weeks. They kissed and held each other tight for several minutes.

"This man freed us," she said after their reunion ended. "We have fifty warriors. The rest were sent back with the people to start rebuilding."

"We rest here tonight," Ethan said. "Then we ride for the castle in the morning."

Ethan let Ulysses and Kenneth plan out their camp, assign troops their tasks and set up the rotation for sentries for the night.

Ethan could not rest. He was not sure how long he lay in his bed looking at the top of his shelter before he rolled out and put his boots back on. The destruction around them turned his stomach. Alaric had to be stopped. He left his tent and stretched. He watched the guards Ulysses placed for the first watch for a moment and then walked to the edge of the village.

Cool air greeted his face. Light from the stars twinkled brightly in the clear sky. From the corner of his eyes he saw the flames from the campfires flicker. Looking around, he saw the silhouettes of two of the sentries.

The others he did not see. Elves were much more adept at remaining unseen. Atherton on the other hand could disappear when he wanted to. A talent the king had learned to appreciate a long time ago.

Ordinarily Ethan used walks on nights like this to clear his head. Not tonight though. The longer he remained awake the more his problems weighed on his mind.

He sensed a presence behind him. Mina's light touch tickled the back of his neck. He smiled. Her touch always lightened his mood.

"Can't sleep?" she asked.

The king shook his head. "No. I'm trying to figure out how to save the kingdom. You?"

She did not answer right away and dropped her gaze. He could tell right away something bothered her. He let her have a moment or two while she collected her thoughts. Shadows jumped on her face as light from the campfire flickered against the dark. He thought for a moment he saw a single tear glisten down her cheek.

He placed a finger under her chin and gently raised her head. "What's wrong?"

The flood of tears spilled all down her face. "I was so angry at you at first but the last few years guilt has eaten me from the inside out." She paused. "Perhaps that is why I hid behind Vanacore so long."

He waited for more but it did not come. "Guilt for what?"

She looked him in the eyes. "For trying to kill you. And for siding with my father in his attempt to take Eden."

Tears flowed down her face again.

Ethan pulled her in close and just held her. She pressed her face against his chest and sobbed. He let the silence take hold between them as she cried. They remained in this embrace for several minutes until her tears stopped. She pushed away and looked up at him.

"I know I don't deserve it but do you think you could ever forgive me?" she asked. Desperation now looked back at him.

He smiled at her. "I forgave you a long time ago. It is about time you forgave yourself."

She fought to return his smile through her tears. "I hope someday you could love me again like you used to."

"I never stopped loving you." He kissed her soft lips. In that moment he forgot all about Alaric Krollnoss and the Najera. It was just a man and a woman sharing a moment under the stars.

chapter 20

Ethan broke camp early in the morning and they rode hard to his childhood home. The sun was high in the afternoon sky when Ethan and his small army arrived at Bekah. The time had arrived for Ethan to confront the impostor who sat on his throne and claimed to be Elyon.

He liberated Tilibra for King Maras. It was time he liberated Eden from the hands of Krollnoss. Somehow he knew a fight with the Najera would follow soon enough. Defeating the sorcerer was the key to protecting every kingdom.

Ethan trusted Elyon would win the battle. The king assumed that Alairic would be as strategically minded as his brother, Xestes was. He expected Alaric Krollnoss to have fortified the castle. He also expected to not have to lay a hand on Alaric or any soldier. Elyon would return the kingdom to the rightful heir and he had given Ethan the instructions to follow.

King Lyons rode with his head held high as he approached his home. Castle Bekah was locked up tight. Closed gates and guards posted on the walls made it clear that Alaric did not want visitors. Ethan did not care. He planned on seeing the sorcerer one way or the other.

About seventy-five warriors followed the king. The Tulchin leader had sent most of his people home to rebuild their village but Kiat and Hennisus remained with Ethan and rode on his right. Ulysses, Atherton and Kenneth rode on the king's left. Mina rode on Ethan's right with the elves. No matter what he said to her, she refused to leave the king's side.

Ethan's army consisted mostly of Tulchin warriors but included a few centaurs from Ulysses' village. Commander Amyx had also returned with them. Gerard had met up with them after seeing his wife to a safe house near the border of Eden in Tilibra.

Alaric commanded the entire army of Eden. Most of those soldiers lived and served in units throughout the kingdom but the number of men he had available in the area outnumbered Ethan's little army three to one.

The king was happy to see Commander Amyx but was saddened to hear none of the other men who were on the beach the morning of his abduction survived. There were a few men with him that he had recently fought with or had left Eden's army once Krollnoss began demanding to be worshipped. Ethan took a deep breath and prayed for Elyon's favor.

Alarm bells rang out from inside the castle walls as they neared. More men appeared on the walls like wraiths in the night. He glanced at Mina her worried face betrayed the weak smile she flashed when she caught him looking

"Everything will be okay," he told her.

Ethan stopped his men just outside the range of the enemy's bows. He chose Atherton to accompany him further to the castle. He chose the guardian to go with him because he knew Atherton would be able to get them out in a hurry if need be.

As neared the castle, the bald mercenary, Roland, appeared on top of the wall.

"I wish to see the king," Ethan shouted.

"The king is not taking visitors today," Roland replied. "Be gone before I release the full might of the palace guard."

Ethan knew the strength of the palace guard. Only the best and the strongest of the army were chosen to protect the king and the castle. He did not want to fight his own elite guard. They were his men and he did not want have to hurt any of them. Today there would be no fighting though. Ethan would see Alaric and tomorrow he will be back on his throne. Alaric will be defeated.

"He will see me. I come with a challenge."

"You dare challenge your king?" Roland shouted back.

"No, I've come to challenge a god," Ethan replied.

Roland stood quiet and without his usual wicked grin. The man disappeared as quickly as he appeared.

Moments later the gate rose and Roland met them with several guards. Ethan found it strange to be led at the point of a spear through his own castle. Roland led them through the castle and into the throne room where Alaric Krollnoss sat smug and confident on Ethan's throne. His disguise still intact.

Ethan observed that simply regaining his memory did not break the spell over Alaric. The sorcerer still looked like Ethan and Ethan looked nothing like himself. Servants he had known for years did not recognize him.

He decided to worry about that later. Right now he had to focus on convincing Alaric to accept his challenge. If Ethan proved to the people of Eden the sorcerer was not Elyon as he claimed, then the time would come that the people would not believe Alaric was Ethan Lyons either. He would be restored to his throne.

"Well, I guess I should not have wasted all of those resources searching for you." Alaric sneered. He turned to Prador, "You were right brother our prey came to us."

Prador beamed at the compliment. "His honor is his weakness."

Ethan took a step back. He did not expect to see Prador here. When they did not find him with Trian, he wondered where they should look for him. He would have never guessed to look here. He called Alaric brother.

Is he another brother of Xestes?

The sorcerer turned his attention back to Ethan. "Where's the traitor Vanacore?"

The king gathered his thoughts. Prador's appearance distracted him for a moment.

"He no longer exists." Ethan thought it best to move the conversation away from their escape.

"I should have the guards seize both of you," Alaric said folding his arms across his chest.

Ethan ignored the remark. "I have a challenge for you, majesty."

"I have already proven myself. I have no need to accept your challenge."

Arrogance ran in the Krollnoss family. Xestes had an issue with it and it would be Alaric's undoing as well. He needed to surround himself with people who acknowledged him for who he wanted to be. His audience would become Ethan's. The soldiers, servants and petitioners would witness the challenge and force his hand.

"People of Eden, I have spoken to Elyon's prophet. He has assured me that this man is not Elyon. He does not even speak for Elyon," Ethan said as he pointed at Krollnoss. "He is just a man."

"Blasphemy!" Roland shouted. "He brought the Tudyck child back from the dead."

Ethan heard the onlookers murmur their agreement.

"I saw it with my own eyes," one servant said from behind him.

Ethan nodded. "The prophet told me he would claim that. You don't have to be a god to do that. I have seen the prophet raise the dead as well just using the power of Elyon's name."

Jonathan Prador, dressed in purple robes smiled at Ethan. "You don't have to take this brother," he said as he climbed the steps to stand next to Alaric.

"Seize the blasphemer," Alaric said with ice in his voice. "Remove his head."

Soldiers grabbed Ethan. He did not resist and allowed them to grab him. Atherton made the next move. The guardian shrugged and the cloak dropped to the floor. His majestic wings sprang forth and light filled the room. The guardian drew his mighty sword. Flames engulfed the hefty blade. Every remaining palace soldier froze.

"Seize them both. This is only an illusion!" the sorcerer shouted. Still no one moved, not even the mercenary Roland.

Ethan smiled. He knew the truth. The others seemed to know the guardian was real and nothing about his wings or burning sword was illusion. The hands that grabbed Ethan loosened their grip. He shrugged them off and then stepped forward confidently. He pointed at the fake king. He thought he saw the man shake a little. *He should fear Elyon.*

"I challenge you to build two altars. Tomorrow at dawn we will meet in the fields outside of the castle. Bring as many worshippers as you can find." Ethan paused to ensure every ear heard his next words. "If you bring fire down from the heavens that completely consumes the sacrifice, then I will worship you as will all of Eden—,"

Alaric smiled. "I accept your challenge."

Roland stepped up to his master. Ethan heard what the bald mercenary asked even though he tried to whisper the question discreetly. "How can you accept a challenge to a contest that you do not know the consequences if you lose?"

"I do not need to know about any consequences because I will not lose," Alaric whispered back.

Prador stepped up. "Brother, the mercenary is right. We should hear the entire challenge before agreeing to it."

Alaric turned on them and raised his voice. "How dare either one of you question me. I am the king. I accept the challenge." He turned to face Ethan and even swaggered down the steps of his dais. His forehead nearly touched the challenger's when he stopped. "Tomorrow you *will* worship me."

The move did not intimidate Ethan in the least. "That is mighty brave, O king, because if you lose, you are to renounce your throne and your claim of being Elyon," Ethan replied.

Alaric's eyes narrowed. Ethan knew the other would not back out of the agreement now, even if he wanted to. He so brashly declared his victory already that he had no choice. He had to participate in the challenge or face humiliation.

Ethan knew the sorcerer would not just give up however. He knew the man would find a way to convince people of his power. Especially with Jonathan Prador as his brother. A master of illusion as an ally could go a long way in his campaign to make others believe.

Ethan smiled as he backed away. "I will see you at dawn." He picked Atherton's cloak up off of the floor and tapped the guardian on the shoulder. Atherton folded his wings together so to not hit anyone or anything. They turned simultaneously to leave. No one tried to stop them as they made their exit. No one even approached them. Anyone in the pair's way simply stepped aside and allowed them to leave.

No one challenged them as they made their way through the halls of the castle. They silently walked unobstructed across the courtyard.

"That is a bold challenge you made, Ethan," Atherton said.

"Sometimes all you need is a little boldness to act and Elyon will do the rest."

"How are you going to explain things when he, looking like the real you, is banished?" Atherton asked as they strolled out of the gates to their waiting horses.

"I am not sure just yet. Sometimes I feel like Elyon is making this up as we go."

Atherton smiled as he mounted his horse. "Elyon is just showing you the path as you go along. Trust me, He has had this planned out for a very long time."

chapter 21

Alaric watched as Lyons and the guardian left. He looked to his brother and Roland. "Follow me," he commanded.

Alaric stormed to the study with the two men following behind him. Jonathan closed the door and Alaric shouted in frustration as he sat down behind the desk. Silently he sat for a moment then he exploded in a flurry of arms as he swept the books, papers and inkwell from the top of the desk onto the floor.

"How dare this man to challenge me in such a brash manner! Who does he think he is?"

"How do you intend to win this challenge?" Roland asked. This was the first time the mercenary ever questioned his ability.

"How dare you question my brother in such a manner?" Jonathan said as he stepped toward the bald man.

Roland drew a knife and smiled his wolfish smile. Alaric thought for a moment that he would allow Jonathan to kill the mercenary. After all, he was not completing any of the tasks that had been laid out for him. Calm came upon the sorcerer as a plan formed.

He stood and raised his hands. "Enough! I cannot have the two of you fighting each other right now."

Jonathan bowed his head and stepped back. Roland sneered and slid his knife back into its sheath.

"What is your plan, brother?"

"Build the altars," Alaric said.

"Alaric, I don't think—," Roland began.

The sorcerer pointed a finger at the mercenary. "I don't pay you to think. *You* do as I say. Build the altars. Let me worry about the magic."

Roland bowed his head in submission. "Yes, majesty."

Alaric waited a moment before continuing with his instructions. He knew exactly the spell to use. He knew how he would win this challenge.

"After you have built the altars, place the driest wood and brush on mine. When the altar for Lyons is complete, pour water on it. Pour water on it all night long. Soak the wood for the sacrifice in the water."

Jonathan smiled. "Brother what if just before the challenge you up the stakes and tell the servants to pour a barrel of water on your sacrifice only it will be lamp oil instead?"

Alaric shared his brother's smile. The man had the heart of a warrior but the head of a ruler. Alaric often thought it a waste that Jonathan wanted to be a soldier like Xestes.

"Yes we will do that as well."

"What if that is not enough?" Roland asked.

Alaric glared at the man for his doubts. He sat down behind the desk.

"It will be enough. Jonathan will use his ability to create illusions to enhance the fire I will create. Lyons will not have an opportunity to do anything."

"If he does?" Jonathan asked.

Alaric became annoyed that now his brother seemed to question him, especially after having such a brilliant idea. As he thought about it he realized that Ethan Lyons had seemed to be very lucky or resourceful. Every trap Alaric had set for him, Lyons had escaped.

"Have Beresth and his men at the ready. No matter what happens. Kill Lyons."

chapter 22

The real king of Eden had not slept well through the night. He spent much of it in prayer. His prayers focused mostly on worship of Elyon. He also sought further wisdom concerning his next course of action. He began to doubt that he really heard from Elyon. He questioned if his challenge came from his mind or from his God. Either way he dared not turn back now.

Ethan stepped out of his shelter for some fresh air. He breathed deep and enjoyed the fresh spring smells of the grass in the field and wildflowers along the tree line of the forest. He quickly became overpowered by the scent of the horses as the wind shifted slightly. He looked up at the moonless night and again asked Elyon for direction.

Movement caught his eye across the field. He shook his head at the sight. Alaric was so desperate to hide the truth of his deception that he placed guards around the twin altars.

He presumed the guards were posted to keep him from tampering with Alaric's altar. Or to keep him from noticing the water that had been poured on his. Ethan chuckled. He had watched castle servants pour barrels of water over one of the altars in between his times of prayer and the short time he had spent sleeping.

He didn't have to look but merely felt the presence of the wild haired prophet next to him. Ethan reached his hands to the sky in a long stretch before he acknowledged the man's presence.

"The sun will be up soon. Aren't you a little early to be bringing your assurances from Elyon?"

"I always arrive when the master means for me to."

Ethan turned to face the cheery man. Ethan could never figure out how the man looked like he was always happy.

"Are you ready to defend the honor of Elyon today, Majesty?" the prophet asked.

Ethan looked at the man and said, "Elyon will defend His own honor today."

The prophet nodded. "You are aware that Krollnoss intends on killing you regardless of the outcome?"

"Yes, but what is it you always say? 'No weapon can stand against me, if I stand with Elyon'?"

"Good. You have listened to me. You have come a long way since I first met you in that desert."

"Elyon has seen me through a lot," Ethan said.

"Believe Him and He will continue to see you through."

The camp began to stir. The king's men emerged from their tents. Atherton approached the king. Ethan glanced to his left where the prophet had once stood. He was no where to be seen. Ethan had become accustomed to the sudden entrances and exits the prophet made. Although this seemed like an important enough matter for the prophet to stay for. Ethan had also become accustomed to the prophet allowing him to fight his own battles.

The king shrugged the thought off as Kenneth and Mina stood where he had expected to see the prophet standing. He stepped forward and looked out over the roughly seventy-five men, elves and centaurs who stood with him.

"Alaric is not to be trusted," he said loudly. The silent gathering hung on to his every word. "When Elyon answers the challenge and He will, Alaric will no doubt order for me to be killed. I do not know how many will act on the order. If any man attacks you, defend yourself but try to spare your opponent's life. These people are your friends, neighbors and brothers in arms. They are only deceived."

He turned his back to his troops and looked into the eyes of his friends one by one. Ulysses' face was the same as always, expressionless and as hard as granite. Atherton looked calm and ready. Anger filled Kenneth's face. Surely his thoughts were of revenge against the false king. Gerard, Kiat and Amyx had the look of the willing soldier waiting for orders.   Only Mina looked concerned. He gave her a reassuring smile and then turned back to his soldiers. As the sun's first rays rose from behind him, he commanded his troops to move forward.

He and his men marched toward the designated area of the field. As they drew closer to the perimeter, the guards Krollnoss posted, snapped their spears into position toward the small army.

"Go no further," one of the men said. He was young with pale blonde hair, skin to match and green eyes. He looked as if he had never even been in a fist fight. The king heard the fear that laced the young man's words and signaled for his men to stop.

He spotted Krollnoss and Roland riding from the castle. Prador and a very large, black centaur followed. Several minutes passed as they trotted to the field. A large group of onlookers followed them. Many of the women carried bouquets of flowers.

The Krollnoss brothers and the large black centaur stopped only a few feet from Ethan. The king could have lunged at Alaric or his brother and pulled them off of their horses. The thought crossed his mind to do just that. He could have killed them both and resolved this matter right now.

Ethan then thought about the importance of this challenge. People would need to see the proof of who Elyon really was. Ethan *could* reach out and kill the brothers but he needed to complete the challenge.

Those deceived by the sorcerer would see him as a martyr if Ethan just killed the man. Witnessing Elyon's miracle today should be just what was needed to break Alaric's hold on the people of Eden.

"It's good to see you again, Deweago," Prador said.

This was the first time Ethan had been this close to Jonathan Prador since the betrayal that cost the life of

Meldorn. He struggled but contained his anger. Killing Prador would not help his cause any. He had to concentrate and focus on the task at hand. Elyon would punish the man for his actions at another time.

Alaric dismounted and stepped up to the king. The Najera medallion dangled around his neck. Ethan thought he saw the face of the rider he had already defeated in the gem. Krollnoss' confidence bordered on arrogance. Although, walking in arrogance seemed to be a natural state for the sorcerer.

"Are you ready, majesty?" Krollnoss whispered. The impostor turned to the gathering crowd behind him. "Today we will settle who Elyon is. Today the world will know what I say is true."

Ethan shook his head at the theatrics. He knew Elyon would show up. He also knew Krollnoss planned to kill he and his friends no matter what. He trusted Elyon would keep them safe. He refused to respond to the other's words. He allowed the sorcerer time to continue with his theatrics.

"The challenge today is to bring fire from the heavens to burn the sacrifice. The victor will be Elyon's spokesman." He turned back to Ethan.

"You may go first if you like," Alaric said as he motioned to the dual altars.

"You go first, Alaric. I insist." Ethan replied.

The other scowled at the sound of his real name. The sorcerer bowed his head a moment in a stance meant to make him appear humble. He turned to the crowd and raised his hands in a grand gesture, spreading them wide apart.

"I wish to show the true power of Elyon. Bring me a barrel of water. Pour it on my altar," he commanded.

He looked at Ethan with the predatory smile he had flashed in the dungeon. The servants did as he commanded. Ethan could smell the lamp oil from where he stood. *Clever,* he thought. The flowers in the women's bouquets helped disguise the odor of the oil. Ethan shrugged. Elyon would still prevail today.

"Those faithful to Elyon pray and fire will come," Alaric said loudly.

He faced the altar with dry wood doused in oil. He nodded and a priest brought a lamb prepared for a sacrifice. The prayers from the crowd became audible and grew louder. Nothing happened. Krollnoss glanced at Prador then at Roland.

"Maybe the prayers need to be louder," Ethan mocked.

Alaric stared hard at the altar. The prayers grew even louder. Alaric raised one hand. Ethan saw it as more posturing. Still nothing happened.

Ethan laughed. "Maybe if you wiggle your fingers," he said pointing his fingers toward his adversary and wiggling them quickly. People behind him chuckled. Ethan noticed both Krollnoss and Prador stood with eyes closed.

Smoke arose from under the dry wood and kindling. A few tiny flames began to lick the sacrifice. Then a quick burst appeared and the sacrifice began to burn.

A gasp of awe sounded from onlookers on both sides. Then the flames grew higher and completely engulfed the sacrifice. Cheers erupted from among the deceived followers of the sorcerer.

The sight did not impress Ethan. Krollnoss glared at Prador. The silent communication between the brothers revealed the truth to Ethan. Alaric used his magic to start the fire and his brother used illusion to expand the flames and make them look impressive. Ethan knew the people would see the real fire if a hard breeze blew.

Alaric must not be as powerful as he wants everyone to think, Ethan thought.

A moment later the flames leapt to the sky almost as tall as a man. People jumped back as it did. Ethan felt the heat and became concerned that he may have been wrong about the brothers. Some of the onlookers knelt at the show of power.

Ethan closed his eyes and calmed his spirit. *This is all part of the illusion,* he told himself.

When he opened his eyes he saw through the illusion into the heart of the fire. The wood was only beginning to char and the sacrifice remained. What the sorcerer conjured was nothing more than a small campfire.

All he had to do was take Prador out of the situation and everyone would see Alaric for the fraud he was. If the king actually did that he would steal the honor from Elyon. His goal for today was to bring honor to his God. The only way to do that is to let Elyon win the challenge.

He acted a little impressed to give his presentation a little dramatic flair. A chant started of "Long live King Ethan." He made no effort to encroach on the moment.

He actually smiled at the thought of the people chanting his name for the sorcerer. He knew the chant had to be driving the impostor mad. The sorcerer raised his hands to quiet the chants.

"That is enough. I think we have proven who Elyon is already but in the spirit of fairness," Krollnoss said. He turned to face Ethan with a wicked grin. "It's your turn."

Alaric motioned toward the other altar. A priest brought the already prepared sacrifice. Ethan was certain the sacrifice had been tampered with in some way. He guessed it had soaked overnight in water. It did not matter much to him though. He knew Elyon would prove the truth in overwhelming fashion. No one would dispute who Elyon was after today.

Ethan stepped up to Alaric's burning altar. He knew illusion fueled part of this fire. He reached his hands out and felt the warmth of the flames. He nodded to his opponent to acknowledge the spectacle was real enough. Then he circled his altar. He looked at the soaked ground surrounding it. He inspected the drenched wood that lay under the lamb. There would be no way for him to start a fire with these materials.

"I am so glad that you are doing this, my Lord," Ethan whispered to Elyon. He turned to the crowd. "Bring me seven barrels of water and pour them over the altar," he commanded.

No one moved. Shocked gasps sounded from among his followers. Ethan looked to Krollnoss to issue the command.

Alaric smirked and waved a hand to the servants who scurried away for the water. It took several men to carry each large barrel. The servants took more time than Ethan wanted them to in order to carry out the order but they fulfilled his request. He liked the result of the additional water poured on the altar but was not satisfied. He called for seven more barrels. Alaric laughed in his arrogance as he repeated the order.

Water flowed from the last barrel and Ethan was satisfied. Water dripped off of the rocks. The wood looked more like rotted pulp than sturdy kindling. A vulture would not have touched the soaked carcass of the lamb. A puddled moat surrounded the altar as the ground could hold no more moisture.

Hushed laughter came out of the crowd of Krollnoss followers. Concerned whispers could be heard from among Ethan's small army. The real king knew the deceived followers of Krollnoss mocked him. Still he did not care. In a moment all would know who Elyon was. All would know the sorcerer for the fake he was. Elyon would defend His honor.

Without further fanfare, Ethan knelt off to the side of the altar. He took a spot away from the soaked ground. He did not want to be caught in the flames he knew would come. Or be accused of some manner of trickery. He bowed his head and said a simple prayer in a voice so quiet all others had to stop speaking for him to be heard.

"Lord Elyon, only you are all powerful. Show them your glory. Send the fire."

Ethan raised his arms together to the sky and then apart quickly. Fire fell from the heavens. The crowds gasped as one. The column of flame consumed the water drenched altar. The flames seemed to pour out of the sky like a waterfall rolling down the mountainside.

Without standing he pointed at the other altar. The fire arched through the air and fell on the sorcerer's altar surrounding it completely. Every rock on both altars burned.

Ethan remained in this position on his knees with arms spread wide. He allowed the fires to burn. No one laughed or murmured. The only sound to be heard was the roar of the fires as they consumed the wood and sacrifice. Finally the king dropped his arms.

The twin infernos extinguished immediately. Nothing remained of either altar. All was destroyed by the fire. Flesh, bone, wood both wet and dry, even the stones of the altars burnt to ash. Not a trace of water around Ethan's altar remained.

Slowly Ethan stood. One by one the crowd knelt around him. He stared at Alaric. The man no longer looked like Ethan. Now Ethan saw the resemblance to his father's killer. Dark eyes, slick, black hair that ended at a widow's peak on his forehead, just like Xestes Krollnoss. The sorcerer had been exposed as the liar he really was.

Alaric, Prador and Roland turned to run. They stopped mid stride as an army rode onto the field from the East, led by three hooded riders. Panic swept through the crowd of onlookers. Chaos broke out as people stood to run. People collided with others as they tried to escape. They pushed older folks to the ground to flee. Parents picked up their children. Even many of the mighty palace guard ran away, afraid to face this new threat.

chapter 23

Kenneth jumped into the fray and tried to bring order to the mass exodus. The king noticed Ulysses had locked eyes with the large centaur. Their gaze broke when the darker centaur turned and ran off of the battlefield..

Ethan knew right away who approached. The remaining Najera arrived. This confrontation was also inevitable. He ran to Ulysses who pulled the bow made to destroy the Najera from off of his back.

"Get these people to safety," the king commanded as he took the weapon from the centaur.

Two of the Najera stopped and the army halted their advance. The third hooded rider trotted forward. It stopped twenty yards or so in front of what remained of the gathered crowd and dismounted. Unseen armor clattered as it took two steps forward.

The creature could easily have looked Atherton square in the eyes. In fact it may have had to look down slightly to do so. The rider pulled back its hood and exposed a hairless wolflike head. Pale skin covered the head. Fangs dripped a mixture of blood and drool. The fingers ended in sharp curved claws. The creature looked like it had stepped straight out of a child's nightmare. It roared and the remaining crowd scattered.

Ethan turned to see that only his closest friends stood with him now. He nocked an arrow. He felt someone suddenly cling to his back. Mina's breath warmed his neck. Tears dripped from her eyes onto the nape of his neck. He closed his eyes to focus.

The king opened his eyes and time seemed to slow when he looked in the faces of those around him. Krollnoss and Prador cowered on their knees. Roland, Gerard and Kenneth all appeared frightened. The large black centaur had disappeared. Kiat and Hennisus readied their weapons nervously. Atherton as usual did not flinch but the normally stone faced Ulysses showed very slight signs of fear.

The guardian stepped forward and peeled Mina off of Ethan's back. The king raised the bow and pulled the string taut. The creature roared again but this time it sounded more like a shrill scream. The sound startled Ethan and the arrow flew wide striking one of the soldiers at the front of the supernatural army in the neck. It withered to ash like the center of a burnt out campfire.

Ethan quickly launched a second arrow. This time his aim was true. The arrow flew straight to where the rider's heart should be but the dreadful creature deflected it with the serrated edge of a wicked looking sword. Another shriek escaped the rider's mouth. Almost as if it taunted the king.

Down to one of the specially blessed arrows, Ethan became concerned. He set the final arrow in place and sprinted toward the rider. A few feet away he dropped to his knees, slid and drew the bowstring back at the same time. It would not be his best shot but he did not think he could miss at this range.

He released the arrow. Ethan held his breath. Again the arrow flew straight. It grazed the neck of the creature. Smoke rose from the wound. The rider screamed again. The king shuddered. His heart pounded so hard against his chest, he thought it would break through. Fear crept into his mind and spirit.

He forced the fear back and scrambled to his feet. No other plan of attack came to mind other than to attack. He ran at the rider.

With one hand on the wound on its neck the other hand batted Ethan to the ground like swatting a fly. The king fell back a few feet and landed hard on his back. He lay still for a moment or two as he struggled to catch his breath. His heart pounded louder. He barely heard his name being called out.

The rider now attacked. Ethan rolled out from under the creature's feet. Fear stomped the ground where the king's head just laid. Suddenly he rolled in the opposite direction, toward the rider. The action surprised Fear and caused the Najera to trip.

Ethan sprang to his feet. He spotted the remains of the second arrow. He ran to it and grabbed it. He turned to see Fear already back on its feet. Ethan held his arms at his side. He clenched the center of the broken arrow with the arrowhead pointed behind him. He ran at Fear, raised the arrow above his head and jumped. As he jumped he brought the hand with the arrow down in a stabbing motion. Again the rider brushed him aside.

Again Ethan found himself on the ground. This time the rider wasted no time. It grabbed the king by his leather vest and pulled him to his feet. The creature stared at Ethan like it was sizing him up. Finally the rider spoke.

"I know what frightens you in the night." It sounded more like the low growl of a wolf rather than spoken words.

The creature howled as the muzzle retracted. Clawed fingers stretched in an unnatural manner before shrinking to human fingers. Hair filled in on the creature's head. With the transformation complete, the king stared back at himself. He smiled and cracked the rider in the head with the bow.

The weapon splintered. Fear shook off the strike and released another bone chilling scream. The rider clutched Ethan's throat and lifted him off of the ground. The king dropped the remnants of the bow as he clawed at the grip now closing his throat. Ethan kicked at the Najera but the creature did not even flinch.

The rider's callous eyes widened. It seemed to take pleasure in the dread spreading through the king's mind. Ethan's body started to tremble. He struggled to break Fear's grip on his body and mind. He knew he had to do something quick.

His fear turned to terror as he could not draw in air. The rider's talon-like fingers dug deeper into his throat making it nearly impossible for Ethan to breathe. He closed his eyes and the darkness of unconsciousness began to envelope him.

He often thought the last thing he would see before he died was a vision of his parents. Instead he saw a vision of himself fighting himself. Then he realized what he saw was not a vision but a memory. Before he became king he fought a shape shifting creature who also sensed a person's fear. His last vision would be of that battle. A battle where he faced his greatest fear and won.

He had already defeated his fear. The rider's grip loosened slightly. Elyon always fought for him so what did he really have to fear? Air flooded Ethan's lungs. He had no reason to be afraid of anything. Ethan opened his eyes again and looked in the rider's eyes. The creature released the king. Its power had been broken.

Ethan remained on his hands and knees, right where the Najera dropped him. He coughed and struggled to take in a deep breath. He wrapped a hand around the broken bow and stood.

"My turn," the king rasped.

Ethan punched the rider with his right fist. Though it did not bleed a gash appeared. Fear seemed dazed after the blow and staggered back. It shook its head then shrieked again and followed that with the full roar. The creature still looked like Ethan. Seeing himself roar like a lion made him pause for a moment.

Fear produced its long sword and ran toward the king. Ethan charged the Najera and jumped toward it. Their bodies crashed together. Ethan's momentum won and he landed on the rider's chest. Fear attempted to raise up from the ground. Ethan quickly wrapped the bow string around the Najera's throat and rolled off pulling as tightly as he could.

The string burned into the rider's neck. Fear clawed at Ethan trying to take hold of the king anyway it could. The king pulled tighter and suddenly fell backward. The rider's head popped off as the bowstring cut all the way through the neck.

Fear's Ethan shaped head fell to the ground. The king trembled at the sight of his head as it rolled on the ground. A moment later the head and body returned to the previous grotesque wolflike form. Both head and body turned to ash.

The wind picked up and blew the ash around. An orange glowing mist swirled and flew toward Alaric. The medallion absorbed the strange mist, just as it happened after Ethan defeated the rider named Famine.

Ethan scrambled to his feet. He faced the other riders. Neither War nor Death moved. Ethan drew his sword. A low rumble issued from under one of the dark hoods.

"Soon," the voice growled.

chapter 24

Kenneth caught a glimpse of Krollnoss and his men as they fled the field. Before he knew what he was doing, his legs started moving. He had began to chase after them. He did not know what he would do if he caught up to them.

They outnumbered him at least four to one. He was sure to die today if he did not stop. Thoughts of Krysta and their son began to run through his mind. What would happen to them if he died?

He continued to run after them. The thoughts of his family ended when he saw Roland glance back at him. The bald mercenary stopped and turned to face him. The others stopped as well. Kenneth saw the mercenary's mouth move but was still too far away to hear what he said.

Alaric and the others began their retreat again. Kenneth smiled to himself and pumped his legs faster. He stopped a few yards from his enemy. Quickly he realized he should have slowed his run sooner. His heart pounded in his chest. His legs burned as he took each wobbly step toward his enemy. He struggled to breathe in his normal pattern.

"I finally get to kill you," Roland said. His hawklike nose and beady eyes made him look much like the creature that Ethan faced.

"We shall see."

Roland drew his sword and a knife. Kenneth responded in kind. The mercenary closed the distance between them with a slash to Kenneth's head. Kenneth ducked and swiped at the other's torso with his knife. Roland jumped back.

Their swords clanged together as they took another slash at each other. Back and forth they attacked and counterattacked. Neither gaining an advantage over the other. Their fluid movements made them look like they were part of an elegant dance, rather than a deadly duel.

The speed of Roland's attacks surprised Kenneth. Only Ethan in their sparring sessions ever struck faster. At the time Kenneth hated those sessions because even though Kenneth was a little bigger and stronger, Ethan always won.

A downward slice caused Kenneth to jump back. Roland followed the attack with a series of left and right slashes with his knife. He attacked again with his sword this time from an awkward angle.

Kenneth took advantage of the misstep and struck down on the mercenary's blade. The weapon fell to the ground. Roland lunged at him with the knife. Kenneth sidestepped the attack and the bald man stumbled forward.

Kenneth stood over Roland with his sword pointed at the man's throat. "Surrender and I won't kill you."

"Why should I surrender to you?"

The question confused Kenneth. "Do you really want to die?"

"You don't have it in you to kill me."

Kenneth stepped forward and thrust his sword closer to the bald man's throat. "I *can* kill you. I should kill you for everything you have done to my family but I won't because Elyon is a merciful God."

"Then that is His weakness and your undoing."

Roland grabbed a handful of dirt and threw it up at Kenneth's face. Next he felt the other's body launch into his. They both fell to the ground with Roland landing on top. Kenneth lost his sword and knife. He coughed and spit trying to get the dirt out of his mouth and lungs.

Though he could not see the move, the shift in Roland's weight on his body told him the man reached for another knife. His sight cleared some and he saw Roland coming down with the knife. Kenneth managed to grab the other's hand to block the strike.

Roland pressed his weight down on the heel of his hand. Kenneth felt his strength begin to fail. He thought of how Ethan defeated him in one of those sparring sessions by using Kenneth's own weight against him. He pulled Roland's knife arm down and pushed it to the left. The knife came down narrowly missing his face. Kenneth bit into Roland's hand. The mercenary did not make a sound but released the knife.

Kenneth began punching his opponent in the ribs repeatedly. Roland stood up and Kenneth scrambled to his feet. He wiped the remaining dirt from his eyes. Roland threw a right hand punch that caught Kenneth on the jaw.

The mercenary spun and kicked his right foot out at Kenneth's face. Kenneth's arms sprang up in time for his hands and forearms to absorb the power of the strike. Kenneth responded with a side kick of his own. His foot landed on the top of his opponent's chest just below the chin.

Roland sprang to his feet and stormed toward Kenneth. He attacked with a series of left and right punches that Kenneth ducked or blocked with his hands. A quick jab to the mouth stunned Kenneth. Roland wrapped his hands around the back of his neck. He jerked Kenneth's head down and brought his knee up to smash into Kenneth's face.

Kenneth managed to soften the blow by getting a hand on the knee. He stood and spread his arms apart, breaking the mercenary's hold on him. He threw a series of three jabs that connected on the hawklike nose of the other. Kenneth twisted his body to the right to avoid a heavy front kick. He threw a right cross to Roland's jaw. Hitting the man felt like hitting a wall at times.

Kenneth jumped toward Roland. Both of his feet smashed into the man's chest. Kenneth landed hard on the ground and he lost sight of his opponent. Kenneth scrambled to his feet.

He heard the ring as Roland unsheathed another knife. The other approached with the blade and obvious bad intentions. Kenneth quickly scanned the ground for one of the other weapons but the fight had taken him away from the other blades they had dropped. He looked up in time to see the blade come at him.

Kenneth tried to step back but was not quick enough. The blade sliced along his forearm. Roland advanced with two more quick slashes. Kenneth dodged the first. He blocked the second and grabbed Roland's wrist.

Twisting the man's wrist, Kenneth pulled him forward and turned. He put his hip into Roland's midsection and threw him over his shoulder. Roland landed hard on the ground. Kenneth dropped to his knees as fatigue from his run took hold.

He fell on Meklin's knife arm near the prone man's head. The mercenary released the blade. Before Kenneth could make another move Roland kicked one leg up and struck Kenneth in the forehead.

Kenneth rocked back and dropped the knife. As soon as Kenneth stood Roland charged him head first. Kenneth locked his arms around the mercenary's head and under one of his shoulders. Kenneth managed to stay upright. He widened his stance and kept the other from pushing him back to the ground.

"Surrender and I won't kill you," Kenneth said.

"If you show me mercy, I will track you down and kill your entire family," Roland said.

His muffled voice did not hide the hate in his words. Melkin reached under Kenneth's forward leg and pulled. They fell to the ground.

Kenneth did not release his grip around the bald head. Roland began to punch Kenneth in the ribs. The pain that shot through his body with each blow made him want to release the madman. The thought that Roland would do what he promised made him hold on tighter.

"Don't do this," Kenneth warned.

The other's response was another punch in the side. Roland then began to reach and feel around Kenneth's body searching for a weakness to exploit. Kenneth felt the other's fingers try to enter his mouth or poke his eyes. Kenneth applied more pressure and pulled up on Roland's neck.

Kenneth felt Roland shift and pull another knife. The mercenary flailed his free arm around with the weapon. Kenneth kept one arm wrapped around the mercenary's neck. He directed the blade to Roland's throat. The blade sunk into Roland's neck.

The mercenary went limp. Kenneth relaxed some and fell back on the ground. Roland's body lay on him. He took a moment to catch his breath. He flipped the lifeless body off of him and onto the ground.

Slowly Kenneth stood. He retrieved his weapons. He looked down at the Roland's body and then at his own bloodstained clothes. He was covered in the blood of the man. Melkin was not the first man that Kenneth had killed. The others were killed during war.

Guilt entered his conscience. His legs trembled and he dropped back to his knees at the sight of what he had done. Tears mixed with the dirt on his face. He did not cry over the death of the mercenary. His tears were tears of shame over the fact that he had killed the other.

Roland was the first man that he wanted to kill in cold blood. He would have done it before had he been given the opportunity. He was ashamed of the lust of wanting to kill the man. Another thought came to him as he asked Elyon for forgiveness.

Roland Melkin was evil. The world was a better place without him. Kenneth told himself he had to kill the man.

If I didn't kill him, he would have kept his promise to kill my family. He left me no choice.

chapter 25

The Najera known as Death and War disappeared after Ethan destroyed Fear. They left no trace that they were even in the field. No prints from either horse or foot soldier remained. Not a blade of grass was bent.

Even the ash that formed when he decapitated the rider had disappeared. It was as if they were an evil vision Ethan had. He knew otherwise though. Everyone present witnessed their evil presence in Eden. The king wished he knew where the riders had disappeared to.

No one actually saw when Krollnoss and his loyal followers escaped or in which direction they had gone. At least no one he knew of. One thing was for certain, they would meet again. And it would be soon.

No one knew where Kenneth was either. The crowd had scattered when Fear exerted its power over the people. Maybe his friend had escaped the scene with the crowd. Kenneth was not the kind to run but Ethan would not blame him if he did today.

Ethan was now home, back at Castle Bekah, where he belonged. Mina had told him that he still did not look like himself. It took Ulysses and the others to convince the castle servants and guards that Ethan was really himself and that Alaric had cast a spell to steal his image.

No one was sure why his face was still hidden. Alaric's disguise had clearly faded. Ethan thought his should as well. The king decided he would worry about that later. Almost everything else seemed back in order. Still he knew this ordeal was far from over. Alaric still roamed the countryside and two of the Najera did as well.

Ethan sat in his private study. His Uncle Rufus used the little unmarked library while he lived at the castle. After Rufus' death and Ethan took the throne, he used the little library instead of the official king's study downstairs. He felt closer to his uncle when he sat in library.

"I could sure use his advice about now," he whispered of his uncle.

King Lyons sat back with his elbows propped up on the arms of the overstuffed chair. His fingers pressed against each other as he pondered where to go from here.

A knock sounded on the door. Kenneth entered with Mina right behind him. His friend made no apology for the interruption. He only smiled exposing all of his teeth. Ethan thought he could even see the ones in the back.

Despite the broad smile, Kenneth did not look good. His black hair held clods of dirt. Fresh cuts over his dark brown eyes and on his chin looked as if they had only recently stopped bleeding. His clothes were covered in dirt and blood. One would have thought he had been stabbed multiple times.

"Are you alright?" Ethan asked.

"Yes, why?"

Ethan motioned at his friend's clothes. "Oh. Most of it is not my blood."

"Do you care to explain?"

Kenneth told the king and Mina how he spotted Alaric and his people running from the battlefield. Mina pointed out how foolish he was to chase them by himself. Kenneth agreed with her and then concluded the story by saying, "I had no choice, Ethan. He said he would hunt down my family. I believed he would have. I had to kill him."

Ethan nodded. "I believe you are right." They let several somber moments of silence go by.

Kenneth made his way around the desk and wrapped his arms around his friend and squeezed. Clearly something excited him. Ethan found it difficult to breathe for a second time today. Only this time he did not know why.

"Choking," the king gasped tapping one of Kenneth's arms.

"Sorry," Kenneth said releasing his grip. He backed up but continued to smile.

"I'm glad you are in such a good mood considering the conversation we just had," the king said after a couple of breaths.

"Why shouldn't I be? My family is safe from a madman, my *real* best friend is back and he brought my sister back to me."

Kenneth went to Mina. She smiled softly as he put one arm around her shoulders and squeezed her in a side hug. She winced as Kenneth put his dirty arm around her shoulders. Ethan smiled. Life almost back to normal.

"Actually, I brought him to you," she said as she pushed Kenneth away after her brother let her go.

She dusted her clothes off. She may have pretended to be a man for the last several years but clearly she still did not like her clothes to be soiled. She crossed the room and sat on the arm of the king's chair.

"Whatever. The point is my family is complete again." He really looked at Ethan for the first time since he entered the room. "Why are you brooding up here? We had a major victory today."

"Yes we did," Ethan replied. "but we haven't won the war yet. Krollnoss is still out there. It is good to know he no longer has an ally like Roland but he still has the medallion."

Kenneth's euphoria quickly vanished and his face turned grim. "And the two most powerful Najera are still loose as well."

"Exactly," Ethan replied.

"Then we have to find Alaric first," Mina said as she stood.

Kenneth thought a moment. "She's right. You can't fight the Najera first. You would just give him their power," he said. "Doesn't he have the other weapons you told us about?"

The king silently nodded. Again he sat back with his elbows propped on the arms of the chair and fingertips pushed together.

"On the other hand we can't just ignore the Najera if they show up," she replied as if Ethan were not in the room.

"The Najera have not shown to be as destructive as we thought. They have yet to attack villages. Other than the two you have defeated they have not lifted a finger to fight. Krollnoss *is* dangerous. He will have almost unlimited power and an infinite army at his command if we go after the Najera first," Kenneth said.

Silence lingered among the three of them for several moments. Then king suddenly leaned forward. "Why is that?" he asked.

"Why is what?" Kenneth returned.

"Why have there not been reports of widespread damage and chaos at the hands of the Najera?" Ethan asked.

"Why did the other two just stand there and not intervene in your fight with Fear?" Mina asked.

"That has bothered me too. They did the same when I fought Famine."

Another silence fell on the room. No one seemed to have the answer to either question. Mina broke the silence with another question. "What are you going to do if they show up again before we get the weapons and medallion back from Alaric?"

"The only thing we can do," Ethan replied. "Trust Elyon."

chapter 26

Not since Alaric was a child had he truly needed someone to shelter or protect him. He often traveled with bodyguards or soldiers. Over the years he used men like Vanacore and Roland as protection and as the killers they were to get what he wanted. If it ever came to a one on one confrontation, Alaric could kill but he liked making others do that work.

Beresth happened to have a safe hideaway not far from the field where he had been defeated. In less than a day he had gone from a king to a vanquished enemy. He loathed Lyons all the more now. He vowed to himself that Lyons would die no matter what happened.

His room was quaint and sparsely furnished. A small bed, table and chair joined the chest of drawers with a bowl and pitcher of water on top of it. He understood why a soldier would need so little. He did not understand why a soldier would need the mirror. He looked at his reflection in the mirror. Lyons' face no longer stared back at him.

I went to all of this trouble for nothing.

Alaric picked up the pitcher of water and began to pour some into the bowl. His eyes caught his reflection again. He slammed the pitcher into the mirror, breaking both. His anger did not stop with the mirror. He turned the chest of drawers over. He took a moment to compose himself after kicking the wall several times.

Alaric stepped out of his room into the square of the centaur's hidden compound. The size of the compound did not impress him. He had seen larger strongholds. In fact he had built larger ones. What impressed the sorcerer was how well hidden the compound was.

Beserth designed the exterior of the compound to look completely natural. Magic and illusion had no place for the centaur. He used the trees, instead of illusion, to camouflage the camp. The stone walls were surrounded by large trees and vegetation all around. The areas where the walls could be seen were unusually low to the ground and looked like piles of stones.

Inside the complex, the buildings were built from mud and logs. The large building in the center of the camp was reserved for Beserth. The compound contained barracks for the troops, an armory, a treasury, a barn and stable and a dining hall.

The camp could hold about eighty troops or fifty centaurs. Usually about two dozen soldiers remained at any one time. According to their host's explanation. Beserth was the only centaur now. Between his other mercenaries and Alaric's men the compound was nearly at capacity.

Alaric looked at the corners of the complex. Watchtowers had been cleverly hidden in the boughs of the tall evergreens. The sorcerer only knew about them because he spotted one of the elves climb into position from inside the compound.

"Brother, the men anxiously wait for your orders," Jonathan said as he approached his brother.

Alaric did not reply. He had not seen Roland since he stopped to fight Lyons' mopey friend. *He had better be dead then,* the sorcerer thought. *If I see him again he will wish he was.*

"Have you seen Roland?"

Jonathan shook his head. "Not since we left Bekah."

Alaric huffed at his brother's word choice. They did not simply leave the castle. They were driven away.

Jonathan interrupted the sorcerer's thoughts. "Alaric, let me fight Lyons. I can defeat him. Better yet I can defeat the Najera."

Alaric looked at his younger brother for the first time since stepping outside. "What makes you think that you can win either battle?"

Jonathan looked offended. "I have trained with the best knights and warriors that money can buy. Besides we have the blessed weapons…" His voice trailed off as if he had forgotten his next words. Jonathan's eyes dropped to his feet. Then he spoke again. "You wish Xestes was here instead of me."

Not this again, Alaric thought.

Greed had been their middle brother's weakness and jealousy had always been Jonathan's. "I told you already, I do wish Xestes was here with us but not instead of you. I wish he was here to be part of our victory. Together the three of us would rule the world."

Jonathan shook his head and pointed his finger at his oldest brother. Beserth approached them. A glance to the centaur told Alaric he enjoyed the sparring match between the brothers.

"No, you wish Xestes were here because you think he was the better warrior," Jonathan said. "You think he could win these battles but you think I can't."

"If I may ask a question," Beserth interjected. "Didn't Xestes already lose to Lyons?"

Alaric dismissed the centaur with a wave of his hand. "You are not necessary right now."

"Fine. I'll get me some wine to enjoy," Beserth said as he turned and walked away.

Alaric turned back to his brother. "Jonathan, each of us had our talents growing up. Ours were in the magical arts. Xestes was always the physical one. You both trained with knights, yes, but he honed his skills on the battlefield."

"There it is. You don't believe in me."

"That is not what I am saying."

Alaric thought hard for a moment. He had to rein in his brother's insecurities. He did not have time to deal with this now. He had to focus on the Najera not his whining little brother.

"You are a fine warrior and a skilled leader of men. However defeating Ethan Lyons or the Najera will take an edge that you do not have."

"Then why do you have the weapons if you are not going to fight the Najera?" Jonathan asked. "You have searched for them for years."

Alaric raised his eyebrows. "Lyons was already supposed to be dead, at least three times. I intended on facing the Najera by arming the best warriors in Eden with the weapons but instead I have had to fight Lyons repeatedly."

"Then give away the weapons."

"What? That is absurd."

"Give Lyons the weapons and let he and the Najera destroy each other."

He considered the notion of giving the weapons to his enemy.

Lyons is expendable.

Hope for his success renewed as another thought came to mind. He would give the weapons away. His enemy would be terminated. Then he would destroy the remaining riders and then use the power of the medallion to eliminate all who opposed his reign.

chapter 27

Alaric liked the idea of Lyons fighting and being destroyed by the Najera but not giving the weapons to him. Supposedly he had destroyed two of the riders already. One the sorcerer witnessed. The other is just speculation but since Alaric now saw two faces in the medallion, he believed the rumors.

No, Alaric had decided, he could not give these weapons to Lyons. He would likely defeat the riders. Over night, Alaric had another idea. A dangerous idea.

Jonathan questioned his brother's sanity. Beserth forced Alaric out of the stronghold after learning of the sorcerer's intention to call the riders. Of course the centaur scoffed at the idea. He did not believe the Najera would be able to be bargained with. No matter how crazy the idea, Alaric was going to try.

"I'll not endanger my men with your reckless whim," the centaur had said.

Alaric allowed the disrespectful tone only because if this did not work then he would still require the centaur's services, especially since Roland was still missing and most likely dead. The sorcerer and his brother hiked through the forest a mile or so away from the hidden fortress.

They left at dawn for the meadow that Beserth told them about. Alaric pressed his brother to walk quickly. He wanted to conclude this business as soon as possible.

While they hiked he considered the merits of his plan. The Najera could certainly just kill he and his brother. Or they could simply refuse to help him, then where would he be? He would be in the same situation as he is now.

The clearing was not very large but it would do for his purpose. Jonathan sat on a large boulder panting.

You can barely breath after hiking a mile and want me to let you fight the Najera, Alaric thought.

He simply shook his head as he went about his work.

"Brother you must be insane. You are the only man alive who is courting death," Jonathan said between breaths.

Alaric only smiled as he reached into his pack to retrieve the supplies he had brought with them.

"I'll do whatever it takes to accomplished our goal and then we will rule the world together, Brother."

Alaric went to work on the preparations for his summoning spell. He mixed several ingredients together and crushed them until he had a fine white powder. He poured the powder in the field. He muttered in another language as he poured.

When he completed the circle, he looked at his brother. Alaric knew his brother's question just by the twisted look of confusion that crossed the other's face.

"It is not for them," the sorcerer said.

"What?" asked Jonathan.

Alaric pointed at the circle. "It is not a trap. The circle is for us when we summon the Najera."

"What do you mean 'for us'?"

"We will stand in the circle as I have created it with a protection spell," Alaric explained.

Jonathan nodded. "So as long as we stay in the circle they can't hurt us."

"Exactly." Alaric stood in the center and motioned for his brother to come join him.

Jonathan stood and walked to his brother. "Do you think this will work?"

"Do I think the protection spell will work?"

Jonathan nodded.

"As long as we stay in the circle."

"Do you think we can bargain with the riders?" Jonathan asked.

Alaric shrugged. He had thought about that. More like worried all night if the Najera would bargain with him, especially since he only had one thing they may be interested in.

"There is only one way to know for certain."

Jonathan's face twisted again as another question clearly came to him. "Will you be able to summon them?"

Alaric grew tired of his brother's questions. He pulled the medallion out from under his shirt and rubbed the jewel. A mist swirled and a face appeared. It was the gaunt face he saw before.

The face seemed to silently laugh maniacally and then it disappeared. The wolf shaped face of the rider called Fear replaced the other. It snapped at Alaric like an angry dog. He feared neither apparition. He knew as long as the medallion hung around his neck, they would not be able to harm him.

The sorcerer closed his eyes and took in a deep breath. He began to mutter more unintelligible words. They were words he did not ever think he would use. A very powerful spell. It was supposed to be powerful enough to summon demons. He began to doubt the strength of his protection spell, but time had run out for him to strengthen it.

The riders called War and Death appeared before them. Only the riders appeared this time. The eyes of their horses glowed red. Their dark hoods covered their heads.

The rider on the red horse dismounted and pulled back the hood. A helmet with four horns on it covered the creature's head. One horn stuck out on each side of the head above the ears. Two formed in the front, almost like they grew from the creature's forehead.

The rider opened its right hand and a large battle hammer appeared. It swung the hammer at the brothers. A kind of green lightning sparked around them as the war hammer crashed in front the brothers. The spell held so far.

The riders laughed. One a deep gravelly tone. The other a high pitched cackle. The cackle from his vision in the village. The other rider removed its hood. Alaric remembered the skull from his vision as well. For a moment he wondered if he faced the destroyer the old man spoke about.

The hammer hit their invisible shield again taking him out of his thoughts of the vision. Jonathan flinched. It became clear that the Najera only toyed with them.

"We have come with an offer," Alaric said.

The mounted rider raised a skeletal hand, "Enough."

War raised the war hammer. It pointed the weapon at Alaric. Despite the fact his protection spell worked the thought crossed his mind that the Najera could still crush his skull with one overhead swing. He pushed the thought aside. He had to focus on his proposal.

"Speak," Death said to him.

Alaric hesitated. He tried to control the shudder in his knees at the sound of the creature's voice. Something told him he would regret this. He pushed that thought aside too.

"I want you to help me destroy my enemy. I want your help to kill Ethan Lyons."

Both riders laughed again. When Death stopped cackling it asked. "Why should we help you?"

"I have something important to you."

"What would that be?"

Alaric glanced to his brother. Jonathan raised the battle ax and sword. His hands trembled holding the weapons up.

"I believe these are the last of the weapons that can destroy you. If you help me I will give those to you."

Neither rider spoke right away. Alaric wondered again if he had made a mistake.

"No," Death said.

He had failed. He no longer had the resources to move against Lyons directly. This was his last chance.

"You have something else we want."

Alaric's ears perked up. "What would that be?"

The bony hand pointed at him. "The medallion and…a sacrifice."

Alaric lifted the medallion from off of his chest. "What kind of sacrifice?"

"Whatever means the most to you."

Alaric considered the offer. He instantly knew what the creature expected as a sacrifice. "I will give you the medallion when Lyons is destroyed."

"Agreed," Death answered.

Jonathan looked over at his brother. "What do we have to sacrifice?"

Alaric stared at Jonathan for a moment. "I'm sorry, Jonathan."

"What? What are you doing?"

"Whatever it takes," Alaric explained.

The sorcerer pushed his brother out of the circle. War grabbed Jonathan by the arm. Alaric's younger brother screamed and twisted trying to flee the grip of the rider. War dragged Jonathan like a child would drag a doll behind her.

Jonathan pounded on the arm and chest of the rider. He kicked and dug his heels into the ground. Nothing stopped the forward motion of War. It stopped at Death's horse.

Death reached down to Jonathan's chest. Its fingers dug into his brother's flesh. Jonathan screamed and cried as the creature's hand entered his chest. Death ripped out his heart. Jonathan stood for a moment. Then his lifeless body crumpled to the ground. Then War and Death vanished before the sorcerer's eyes.

chapter 28

Alaric rode at the head of his new army. Beserth on his left and the Najera riders to his right. In order to secure the centaur's allegiance he was promised a lot of gold and silver once Lyons was dead.

Alaric had agreed to those terms with the centaur before his bargain with the riders. After striking the deal with the riders, Alaric guessed he did not need the centaur and his forces any longer.

Alaric had sacrificed so much already to gain the services of the Najera but decided to honor his arrangement with the centaur. It did not matter to him if a rider or Beserth killed Lyons, as long as the man was destroyed. Alaric had already sacrificed so much time, money and family to see this through. A few more pieces of silver and gold meant nothing to him at this point.

Beserth only had about one hundred of his soldiers behind them. These were the troops who lived in the outpost they hid out in as well as a second not far from the first. Most were men, but there were many centaurs and elves as well.

The real army, the skeleton forces of Death and the orcs and goblins of War, rode or marched behind the Najera. Despite the large numbers they moved quickly and quietly across the fields and through the woods of Eden.

The sorcerer estimated they were only about an hour's ride from Castle Bekah when they spotted their opposition. Lyons rode at the head of the army of Eden. Alaric guessed about one thousand Tulchin riders joined Ethan's army of five thousand men. The sorcerer smiled. His victory today was guaranteed.

"Roughly six thousand," Beserth said breaking up Alaric's thoughts.

"What?"

Beserth turned to the sorcerer. "I am just estimating the size of their army as about six thousand souls."

Alaric nodded. He signaled for the army to stop. He looked at the centaur "With me."

The pair trotted out toward Lyons. The King of Eden stopped his army's march and did the same with Ulysses at his side. Alaric waited for the others to join them.

"Did your brother return home?" Ethan asked.

Alaric scowled. He thought about running a sword through the other right at that moment.

That would end this battle quickly.

Instead Alaric spoke, "I have your army outnumbered three or four to one. Just surrender now and I will let you and your friends live in exile on a nice island far from here."

"I was going to make the same offer to you."

"I have the numbers advantage. Why would I surrender?"

"I have the advantage of Elyon fighting for me."

Beserth snorted. "Show me Elyon, from among your ranks. I want to see how *He* handles a sword," the centaur mocked.

Alaric ignored the comment. "I will give you one last chance to surrender your kingdom, Lyons. As I said before if you do I will allow you and your friends to live and ship you all off unharmed to live in exile."

"We will not surrender. Every man will die to protect this land," Lyons said.

"That is a little dramatic, don't you think?"

"This ends today, Krollnoss," Ethan replied and turned his horse around and rode off. Ulysses walked backwards keeping his eyes on the enemy.

Alaric turned his horse around. "He is right. This ends today," he said to his centaur companion. "You are to kill him today no matter what."

"It will be done."

"So I have been told many times. Let me put it another way. If he walks off of this battlefield, then you don't." Alaric glared at the centaur. There was no real reason that Beserth should have been intimidated by the sorcerer but Alaric tried.

"I've been threatened by more powerful beings and none have succeeded to this point," the centaur scoffed.

Alaric stopped his horse. Beserth stopped next to him. On his horse the sorcerer stood eye level to the large creature. "That is not a threat."

"I've been told that before too." Beserth walked away.

Alaric took his time to return to the line. The black centaur's arrogance and lack of respect angered the sorcerer. He turned his attention to the battle. He looked at the rider called War and nodded.

The battle was to commence. From the top of its red horse the Najera motioned for their armies to advance. Orcs, skeleton soldiers, centaur, elves and men rushed forward at once. Alaric enjoyed the sight of his armies as they moved forward like the waves of the ocean.

Arrows from the Tulchin elves flew through the air. Instead of the usual high flying volley most armies use when they employee archers, the projectiles came in straight at the advancing army. A few of the supernatural soldiers fell but the casualties were mainly among Beserth's troops.

Alaric's army began to run head on toward the army of Eden. The arrows stopped and the army of Eden advanced. When the two armies met the crash thundered across the land and caused Alaric to instinctively look up for signs of a storm. He only saw a clear blue sky.

The serene quiet of the field quickly vanished. Replaced by the clanging of metal against metal. The screams of injured and dying men replaced the songs of the birds.

He heard bones being crunched and shields being split. The smell of blood and other bodily odors overpowered the smell of the wildflower. Alaric saw some of the more inexperienced men on both sides vomit after their first kill. Only a few of them lived to take a second life.

Alaric searched for the King of Eden among the sea of soldiers. Lyons sat on his horse cutting down every opponent that closed in on him. The heads of skeletons and orcs fell with each swing of his blade.

Tudyck and the guardian fought next to their king. He did not see where Ulysses fought but did not care. Beserth could kill them all or not, as long as Lyons did not make it off of the field.

Alaric turned to Beserth. "Kill him!" he shouted above the noise.

The centaur drew his sword. The blade seemed twice as long as any sword Alaric could carry. Beserth marched toward his target. He quickly and ruthlessly dispatched anyone who opposed him. He even lopped off the heads of a few orcs who stood between him and his target.

A few enemy soldiers stabbed at Beserth as he approached the king. He kicked these men away with his rear legs. He started to gallop to Lyons. He raised his sword to strike and swung down. Another blade blocked the attack. Ulysses pushed Beserth's blade aside.

Alaric's army seemed to be falling apart very quickly. So far the army of Eden held its own against his. With the advantage in the number of soldiers on the field, he expected more of his army. Alaric sighed, disappointed with the results so far.

"Send in the dragon," he commanded.

chapter 29

The King of Eden rode back to his position with his men after meeting Alaric in the middle of the field. He watched the other take a place behind his army's lines. Ethan knew Elyon would fight with them today. Still he said a quick prayer asking for favor in the battle.

Ulysses galloped to the other side of the field to lead the men there with Gerard and Commander Amyx. Kiat and Hennisus led their people in the center column. Atherton and Kenneth stood next to the king.

The rider on the red horse signaled for Alaric's army to march forward. Ethan looked to Kiat and signaled for the archers to fire. The Tulchin elves had deadly aim. They fired directly at the oncoming army. Men and orcs fell.

The centaurs continued to gallop with arrows protruding from their muscles. The volleys from the elves cut down some of the enemy numbers but not enough. The king took a deep breath. He signaled for the army of Eden to move forward.

Elf, orcs, men and horses collided with deadly and thunderous results.

Ethan cut down orc after orc. The bodies piled up to the point his horse could barely turn. He barely kept up with the number of creatures that attacked him. Another orc jumped onto his horse. Ethan jammed his blade into its throat. The creature screeched and fell. As quickly as he put one down another took its place. They were like ants on the core of an apple.

Ethan nudged his horse forward with his heels in the animal's flanks. He felt the crunch of bone as the horse stepped on the bodies of the dead. A pair of hands reached up and grabbed the king.

He turned his head to see a helmeted man pull on his chainmail trying to stick a sword under the king's arm. Ethan sliced down on the man's hand. Kenneth finished him with a knife to his exposed neck and threw the body to the ground.

Ethan felt his horse become nervous and unbalanced with all of the bodies around them. He struggled more with keeping his horse steady now than with the enemy.

Kenneth, Atherton and other soldiers protected him. He began to think remaining on his horse was a bad idea. He wanted his men to see he fought with them. The horse turned again in time for him to block an ax from a skeleton. Ethan kicked the undead creature and the skull fell off with the rest of the bones crumbling where it stood.

The king turned in time to see the large black centaur approach. He barely saw the other's blade coming down on him. He braced for what certainly would be a death blow.

Another blade intercepted Beserth's strike. Ethan turned to see Ulysses push aside the weapon. He nodded at his friend. Ulysses forced Beserth away from Ethan.

The king turned back in time to dodge a strike from another skeleton warrior. The blade meant for him cut into the neck of his horse. The animal reared back and Ethan fell off. His horse collapsed onto the skeleton, crushing the bones to dust.

Orcs immediately jumped on him. The king punched and kicked trying to get the creatures off. They swarmed like wolves on a fallen deer. One bit his arm. Another bit him on the leg.

Kenneth and Atherton pulled them off pushing a blade through each orc as they did. When the mob was cleared, Kenneth offered Ethan a hand. As his friend pulled the king up another orc rushed from behind Kenneth. Ethan thrust his sword through this orc. The king lopped off two more orc heads in quick succession.

There was a pause in the attacks around him. Orcs, elves and men looked behind the king. Ethan turned toward the other line to see why.

A dragon rose up from the ground. It stretched its wings and roared at the sky. Dark brown scales covered the creature's body. A series of horns protruded from a ridge on the back of the monster's head.

Ethan had faced many dragons in the year he was a dragon slayer after his father was killed. None of the dragons he faced were as big as this one. Even the legendary Stone Dragon, which was supposed to be the largest dragon to have ever lived, was smaller than this dragon. At least Ethan had killed the Stone Dragon.

"That is all yours, buddy," Kenneth said as he slapped the king on the back.

Despite all of the dragons that Ethan had killed in the past he doubted he could defeat this one. In that moment he wished, Kyros, the king of the dragons would show up.

I guess it is up to me.

"I can do this," he said to Kenneth trying to reassure himself more than his friend.

He took a step forward to run to attack the creature. Atherton stepped in front of him. His sword and snow white clothes stained with the black blood of the orcs. "I have always wanted to slay a dragon."

"Should we be worried about that?" Kenneth asked.

The guardian shrugged off his cloak. Ethan shielded his eyes from the brilliant light that always shined when this happened.

As the light filled the battlefield all other fighting ceased for that moment. When the light ended Atherton stood tall again wearing snow white apparel. He looked like he had never swung his weapon on the field today. The blade on his sword changed from steel to flame. Exactly as Ethan had seen before.

Atherton's wings folded to his back. The dragon roared again and flapped its wings. The guardian also flapped his wings. A moment later both dragon and guardian faced off in the air. The dragon blasted fire through the air. The guardian dodged the blast.

"At least the dragon is not a threat," Kenneth said.

The skirmishes began again. Orcs attacked the friends. They began to duck and stab the filthy creatures. They fought next to each other as always. One helped the other. When one knocked an orc to the ground the other finished it off. Shielded skeletons attacked. They pushed Ethan and Kenneth back with the shields and slashed with their swords and axes.

Ethan managed to take the nearest skeleton down and take its shield. He blocked strikes from other skeletal soldiers and orcs. He smashed the edge of the shield into the skulls of the skeletons and sliced the heads off of the attacking orcs.

The king glanced up at Krollnoss. The rider on the red horse dismounted and removed its cloak. It wore a large horned helmet. The sorcerer handed the black weapons to the rider.

That must be War.

Ethan ran toward the rider.

"Where are you going?" Kenneth shouted as he put down another creature.

"To stop War."

"A little late for that, don't you think?" Kenneth shouted but the king barely heard the quip.

He focused on the horned creature ahead and how to take it down when it carried the weapons Ethan needed to defeat it.

chapter 30

Calmly War strutted onto the battlefield. As Ethan's men or Kiat's elves attacked the Najera, they were swatted away like bothersome flies. It crushed orcs and skeletons from its own army. Beserth's soldiers ran away from the indiscriminate killer. Even the normally fearless centaurs kept their distance from the supernatural creature. Ethan's men cowered and began to run as well.

The rider continued the chase. Squads of men and elves fell, either wounded or dead, with a slash or two of the battle ax or sword.

Most of the men War struck were sliced in two. All the more reason for Ethan to reach the Najera. His army could fight the orcs and other unnatural creatures but he did not know who else could stand up to this dark rider.

Kiat's brother was going to try. Ethan saw Hennisus as he ran to battle the creature as well. He smashed his knotted club on top of the rider's helmet. He swung it from the right and smashed the weapon into the head of the Najera. The creature roared.

Hennisus remained undaunted. He continued to swing his club. Left. Right. Then left again. One blow after another he smashed into the head of the rider. He jumped and swung his club over his head. He brought it down on top of the head of the rider. One of the front horns broke off. The strike seemed to cave the helmet in on itself. Hennisus took one last swing. He swung the club up almost like an upper cut.

The blow sent the rider into the air and onto its back. Orcs swarmed Hennisus. Ethan ran to help the giant elf but stopped suddenly as War stood up again.

It took one swing of the battle ax and brushed Hennisus and the orcs aside. Ethan saw that the blade of the ax had cleaved several orcs in half. He hoped Hennisus did not suffer the same fate. He forced the thought out of his mind. He had to focus on the fight.

Ethan ran to face the rider. He slashed the orcs, men and elves with his sword in one hand and cracked skulls with the shield on the other. He blocked two orc axes at once with the shield. He cut the hand off of one of the filthy creatures and then stabbed the other in the throat. He pushed the handless orc aside with the shield and followed it up with a stab to its chest. He turned to face his anticipated opponent.

Ethan locked eyes with the rider called War. He could not make out many of the features of the Najera's face. Steel surrounded the crown of its head. Two steel horns protruded from the sides of the helmet above where the ears should be. One horn came from the front after Hennisus' attack, with a hole where the other used to be. Plates of metal protected the neck and wrapped around to cover the cheeks. The helmet reminded Ethan of the style the mountain dwarves used to wear.

The king saw a crooked, bulbous nose. A black beard and mustache caked with blood, mud and only Elyon knew what else, surrounded the mouth. The creature sneered at Ethan and showed its yellowed, broken teeth.

War stood shorter than Hennisus and Atherton but was still over a head taller than the king. This rider, unlike the others, was built like a stone wall. Wide and solid. In one hand it carried the blessed sword and in the other the battle ax. Ethan quickly tried to form a plan of attack. Nothing came to him. At least no plan that did not end with instant death for him.

Both weapons looked as if a man would have to wield them with both hands. The rider held the sword like a dagger. It held the ax mid-shaft and swung it like a hatchet. It raised both arms and roared as a challenge to the king.

Ethan adjusted the shield on his arm and slid his sword from the chest of the orc he had just killed. He tried to slow his breathing. His arms and legs already burned from the fight. Sweat dripped along his forehead. The king used the back of his sword hand to wipe it away.

An orc jumped at him from the left. It flailed a pair of axes at him. Easily he blocked the attacks with the shield. He sunk his blade into its thin neck. The dead orc fell at his feet as he yanked the sword out of its body.

War growled something that Ethan could not understand. The rider seemed to have commanded the soldiers to stop their attacks on Ethan. Apparently the Najera wanted to face the king alone. Ethan glanced at the sorcerer. Krollnoss smiled, wicked and arrogant. Ethan could not get over seeing such an evil look on the man's face. The same look Xestes used to give him when his father was not around.

He looked back at War in time to see the rider charge. He ran to meet the monster. The two crashed into each other. Ethan merely bounced off the Najera. He fell back about a foot. He learned his assessment was correct. The rider was as solid as a wall. Just like a stone wall or the side of a mountain.

He lay on the ground to catch his breath.

That didn't work out as planned.

War attacked with an overhand strike with the ax. Ethan rolled out of the way. The blade sank into the dirt to the shaft.

Quit thinking. Get up. Fight!

The king released the shield and scrambled to his feet. He faced the rider with his sword leading the way. The thrust pierced the leather armor of the Najera. The rider only snarled and pulled the ax out of the ground.

Ethan's attack had the impact of an insect biting a dragon. He jumped back to avoid the backhand swing of the ax. He jumped back again to avoid the sword strike that quickly followed.

Ethan slashed down to the left at the rider. His blade only cut the leather of the rider's armor. War advanced and led with the sword. Ethan parried the attack and aimed his own sword at the creature's throat. The helmet hung low enough to stop his attack.

Think. You need a better plan.

Ethan dodged and blocked each blow that followed. He knew that he would tire before the rider. He needed to get one of those weapons away from the Najera. He noticed the dents on the monster's helmet. Marks left by the heavy club of Kiat's brother.

The club may just work for him. He searched around for the weapon. War attacked again. It swung each of its weapons at his head. He ducked after each swing. Ethan tried a counter attack. He slashed at the rider's legs. Again the attack was ineffective. The rider slammed the ax down against the blade of Ethan's sword. The blow forced the weapon out of the king's hand.

Ethan saw Hennisus laying unconscious several dozen yards to his right. The big elf's club laid by his hand.

I can make it.

He sprinted to the elf. He heard the thump of each footfall as the Najera charged after him. He reached the Tulchin first. He looked over his shoulder in time to see the sword fly at his head. The king ducked and rolled forward. He stopped at the club.

Though it was fast for its size, the Najera was too big to stop quickly. It ran past Ethan a few feet before making a complete stop. The king grabbed the end of the club. He struggled to raise it up. It felt like pulling a tree out of the ground with his bare hands.

He stood with his feet wide apart and lifted the elf's club over his head. The weapon felt clumsy in his hands. Partly because Ethan did not use a club. His sword was very balanced and felt like an extension of his arm, but the club felt clumsy because of its size. Hennisus made using it look too easy.

War approached him. His arms grew tired but he had to wait for the right moment to strike. He figured he would only have one chance at this attack. When the rider was close enough, he brought the club down. The head of the club slammed down on the rider's left shoulder and arm. That hand opened and the rider dropped the ax. The Najera swung at Ethan with the sword.

Ethan ducked and rolled forward. He grabbed the ax. From his back he heaved the weapon up. The weapon cut into the side of the creature. The king jumped to his feet. War only roared. Ethan pulled the ax back. His strike barely cut through the leather armor.

Ethan rushed the rider. He used both hands and swung his weapon from over his head. The rider attempted to block the attack with the sword. The force from the king's strike knocked the blade from War's hand. Ethan continued to swing the ax. The Najera simply stepped back to avoid the attacks.

War stopped and seemed to grin. A large war hammer appeared in the creature's left hand. The head of it was made from a stone twice as large as a man's head.

The shaft of the hammer was almost as tall as the king. Ethan attacked again. War blocked the blow with the hammer. Easily it brushed the king's ax aside. Ethan fell to the ground and dropped his weapon. He reached for the handle. War smashed the battle ax's blades with its hammer.

The king scrambled back. He felt the blade of the sword on his right. He kept scrambling back until he reached the hilt. As he began to lift the weapon to attack, War stepped on the blade. It splintered.

The Najera grabbed Ethan by the throat. War squeezed and lifted the king off of the ground. Ethan struggled with his free hand to try and break the grip. He felt his throat begin to close as the Najera's fingers curled inward. His heart pounded. His lungs burned as he tried to breathe. His vision blurred and began to go black.

He remembered the broken sword in his right hand. He poked the Najera's arm but could not muster the strength to do damage. He flailed the weapon around wildly. Blackness almost took his vision. With one last attempt he thrust the blade forward blindly. Then darkness surrounded him as his breath ran out.

chapter 31

Ulysses muscled the bigger centaur's sword aside. He swung his sword with several quick slashes in order to force Beserth back away from the king. Beserth smiled at the change of target. Ulysses knew this day would come eventually.

"You are going to challenge me to protect him, are you?" Beserth held his sword with the blade down and the tip angled back toward his horse body.

"Do you remember what happened the last time you challenged me?"

Ulysses did not respond at first. He circled the other centaur. "I remember you refused to fight me with honor."

"We were thieves. We had no honor."

"You and two others attacked me from behind and left me for dead."

"A mistake that I do not intend to make again." Beserth replied. The dark centaur whipped his sword up and at an angle from right to left. The tip of the blade cut Ulysses along his stomach up to his shoulder. He felt the sting but the wound was not very deep. He would live.

Ulysses slashed at the other's head. Beserth ducked. Ulysses only cut through the air. He swung again and again only cut the air. He slashed down the front of Beserth. He surprised the larger centaur with the attack that resulted in a cut along the body much like the one he received.

Beserth moved in closer for another strike. Ulysses parried it but missed the punch that came in from the left. Ulysses raised his sword in time to block another slash. The power of the black centaur overwhelmed him in his dazed state. His sword flew out of his hand to the left. He stepped back almost tripping over a body behind him.

"Fight me in the old ways," Ulysses challenged.

Beserth snorted as he gave his sword a quick spin at his side. "Why should I put down my sword to fight you with my fists?"

"For honor."

The black centaur chuckled. Contempt and not amusement fueled his laugh. "I don't need honor. I have gold. A lot of gold."

"Gold will not buy back your reputation. Or the honor of your forefathers."

"I have the reputation I want and my forefathers are all dead. If you are so concerned about honoring your forefathers, prepare to join them."

Beserth attacked with an overhand strike with his sword. Ulysses crossed his wrists above his head and trapped the other's arm in his. He grabbed Beserth's wrist, pulled down and twisted the arm to the left. He jerked the arm forward and Beserth dropped his sword. The black centaur yanked his arm from Ulysses' grip.

"I suppose you get your wish, a hand to hand fight." Beserth shrugged his shoulders and rubbed his sword arm. "I can kill you without a blade just as well."

He jabbed Ulysses with his left fist. The punch smashed him in the nose. Beserth's right fist crashed into the left side of his face. Ulysses stepped back. Beserth threw another punch which Ulysses blocked. He countered the blow with a jab of his own that smashed into Beserth's nose.

Ulysses punched Beserth in the stomach and jabbed again to the face. Quickly he followed up with a series of jabs and then an uppercut. Beserth stumbled slightly. Ulysses aimed a punch to the other's throat. Beserth swatted his fist away.

Each centaur punched and blocked the other's attacks for the next several moments. Neither seemed to gain an advantage over the other. Ulysses landed a couple glancing shots to Beserth's body.

Ulysses stopped his attack and stepped back. Beserth stepped forward with a wild swing of his right fist. Ulysses twisted his torso slightly back and to the left. His move threw the other off balance as the blow missed the target. He quickly slid his right arm up and under Beserth's left arm and shoulder.

He wrapped his left arm under the other's chin at the same time he locked his left hand onto his right forearm and his right on the back of his opponent's neck.

Ulysses began to squeeze his massive biceps. He pushed Beserth's head forward. As Ulysses applied the pressure to break his enemy's neck he felt the point of Beserth's elbow strike him in the lower torso. Beserth raised up on his hind legs. His size and strength lifted Ulysses off of the ground. Still the smaller centaur held on.

Ulysses tightened his grip. He tried jerking the mercenary's head back. Beserth was just too strong. Ulysses slipped his left bicep up further under the other's chin. He adjusted his grip enough to go from an attempt to break Beserth's neck to just choke the centaur to death. His arms began to ache from holding on so tightly.

A sharp, burning pain shot through his side and he released his hold on Beserth. Ulysses crumpled to the ground.

chapter 32

Alaric watched in disgust as his army took no real advantage on the battlefield. His men and elves continued to fight but were being held off by the army of Eden. Above him the dragon had yet to attack the enemy. The guardian fiercely fought against the beast. Not only had Beserth failed at killing Lyons he now fought for his own life against Ulysses.

He sat on his horse shaking his head in disgust. Dead orcs lay all around the battlefield. Some killed by Beserth or the rider War. Neither of which seemed to care about the losses. Each warrior killed whatever being stood between them and their target.

Lyons himself hacked through just as many to face War. At least the rider looked to be victorious in the battle against the king. The sorcerer enjoyed watching that battle. Ethan threw himself at the rider to no avail. He slashed at War with no effect. He might as well have struck the Najera with a flower. Now the creature lifted Lyons by the throat and seemed to throttle the king.

Alaric sat up a little straighter on his horse. Victory was at hand. War only had to finish the king off. "Squeeze him! Break his neck!" the sorcerer shouted.

Ethan began to flail his arms wildly. A sure sign of panic if Alaric had ever seen one. In a single unlikely moment, his victory was taken away. In one hand Lyons held tight to the broken sword. Somehow Lyons managed to slash War under the helmet and then wedge the blade under the rider's chin.

A low rumble emanated from the open mouth of the rider. The Najera's body trembled and seemed to break apart like a slab of marble being chipped at by the sculptor's chisel. Then the creature simply fell apart.

A red mist swirled in the place where War had just stood. The mist floated toward Alaric where it was absorbed into the medallion around his neck.

As Lyons crumpled onto the ground after War released him, Alaric glanced to the fight between the two centaurs. Beserth reached a knife on his belt and stabbed Ulysses in the side. The black centaur galloped his way. Anger burned inside the sorcerer's belly. Beserth had failed him a second time.

He looked to the sky. The dragon breathed fire toward the guardian. Atherton's fiery sword absorbed the flames. Atherton whirled the weapon above his head and a burst of flame shot toward the dragon. The mighty beast chased the guardian and snapped at him. Atherton punched the animal on its scaly nose.

The creature roared and chased the guardian more. They looped through the air shooting fire back and forth at each other. Finally the guardian swooped in behind the dragon. Leading with his sword he punched through the skin on one of the wings. A man sized hole tore through the wing of the dragon and the beast shrieked. The ground shook when the dragon fell from the sky crushing several orcs and men.

The guardian floated down from the sky. When his feet touched the ground Atherton folded his wings to his back. He walked to the growling beast. It snapped at him. Calmly the guardian reached the wounded dragon. Twin fireballs shot from the nose. Atherton used his blade to block the fireballs.

The flaming blade carried by the guardian changed back to gleaming silver. Atherton plunged the weapon into the neck of the beast. The dragon lurched and rolled on the ground for only a moment. The dragon finally lay still.

"Retreat," Alaric said.

Beserth met up with the remaining men. He hung his head and hid his eyes from Alaric as he walked past the sorcerer.

"Fall back!" Alaric commanded louder. He turned his horse and led his army away from the battlefield. He swore he would return. He would kill Lyons.

chapter 33

Alaric paced around in Beserth's stronghold. After the defeat and Beserth's repeated failure to kill Lyons, the sorcerer had the leverage he needed to wrestle control of the centaur's network of mercenaries away from him. Alaric stood with the centaur and Death as he planned his next move.

The sorcerer looked at Beserth. "You failed to kill Lyons, again. Why should I let you live?"

"I can kill him," Beserth said through clenched teeth. "If Ulysses had not stopped me, I would have cut his head off."

Alaric glared at his hired mercenary. For the first time Alaric saw fear in the centaur's eyes.

"I did not hire you to give me excuses. I hired you to kill one man!" Alaric shouted raising one finger to emphasize his point.

Beserth hung his head like a scolded dog. Alaric knew the creature could crush his skull with just one of his hands but did not let up on his rant. "Lyons is one man. He is three times smaller than you and yet you cannot put a sword in his gut."

"Roland and Wakenda each failed to kill him," the centaur said.

"And they are both dead."

"Neither of your brothers could kill him either."

Alaric exploded. He stood as close to in the face of the big centaur as he could, with clenched fists, shouted, "Never speak of my brothers again or I will kill you on the spot!"

The sorcerer stepped away to consider his next step. No one spoke for several uneasy moments. Beserth finally broke the silence.

"Let's lay siege to the castle. I will challenge Lyons to a battle of champions. Fighting me alone, he will never be able to beat me. I will kill him this time."

Alaric thought about it. He actually thought that was a good plan. "Alright, but know this, if you fail again then you had better hope that he kills you."

Beserth bowed his head and humbly scurried away with the humility Alaric expected from the centaur and Roland from the beginning.

The sorcerer turned to the last remaining rider. He pointed his finger at the skeletal figure.

"You failed me too. Your army did nothing to destroy Lyons." He shook his head. "In fact three of you failed to kill him."

Death raised his own boney finger. "Our agreement only gave you control of our armies. You failed to lead them effectively." The rider's voice was raspy and it sent chills through his body.

Alaric folded his arms as his wrath built up inside. "You must finish this the next time."

"You can do that yourself. You control the power of the others in the medallion," Death said. "Let me show you how."

chapter 34

Hushed voices welcomed King Lyons to the conscious world. Although he was not so sure which world he would see when he opened his eyes. Ethan thought the rider had killed him. When he opened his eyes he half expected to see the faces of his Uncle Rufus, Meldorn and Elyon himself.

"It's been two days. Shouldn't he be up and moving by now?" a female voice whispered. The words spoken were soft and sounded as if they came from a distance. He thought the voice belonged to Mina.

"He'll be fine. He just needs rest," said a second voice. This one, male and did not try to whisper as much as the first .

Ethan opened his eyes to see a stone ceiling. He woke up in the realm of the living. He looked around and realized he was in his bedchamber. Slowly, he sat up. Mina's voice was the female voice he had heard. She turned her head to face him.

Upon realizing he was alert, she rushed to his bed and sat down on its side. The wild haired old prophet made his way to the other side of the bed.

The prophet held his hands out and spread his arms apart like a magician showing his audience the finale of his performance. "See, he just needed a little more rest."

Mina threw her arms around his neck and kissed him. Ethan kissed her back, happy to be alive. He let her lips linger on his then gently pushed her away. His head throbbed and having her leaning on him did not help with the pain. Beside the pain in his head he had questions he needed answered.

"What happened?"

"You won," Mina said.

"I need a few more details. The last I remember was being choked by War."

Mina leaned him slightly forward and placed pillows behind his back to prop him up. She adjusted the blanket around him.

"Just relax for a moment. I'll send up some food. After you eat and take a bath, you can meet with Kenneth and the others and they will fill in the details."

She kissed his forehead lovingly, stood and walked out of the room. The king turned to the prophet. "Can you provide me with some answers?"

"Of course," the other said with his normally cheerful smile but he did not elaborate on any details.

"Will you?"

"Of course not. You need to eat, rest and certainly bathe. Do as Mina has told you. Relax for now. Kenneth and the others will give you your details."

"If you are not going to tell me what happened, why are you here?"

"Elyon is calling me away. He wants me to remind you that He is always with you and no weapon can stand against you. Keep your faith and rely on him. He will bring you the victory."

The prophet held out his hand. Ethan clasped his own hand around the other's forearm.

"Until next time, Prophet."

The prophet took his leave from the king. Ethan leaned his head back against the pillows behind him and closed his eyes. He did not know how much time had passed between the time he closed his eyes and food was brought in for him.

A servant brought in a large platter with fruit, bread and cheese on it. He wolfed down every bite and washed it down with a half of a pitcher of water. Servants then began bringing in hot water and filling the tub in the room. A servant girl took the empty dishes from his feast.

A male servant helped him out of bed and over to the tub. The king dismissed all of them and began to remove his clothes. He climbed into the tub.

The hot water relaxed his muscles and relieved his soreness. Bruises lined his arms and chest. Mina said they had won the battle but he wondered at what cost. Quickly he finished his bath and dressed to get the answers he wanted.

Slowly he walked down the stairs to the throne room. Everyone waited for him. Mina met him first and slid her arms around his back. She put her head on his chest. Ethan winced and gently put one arm around her. He kissed the top of her head. Silently he thanked Elyon for the chance to hold her again. She released him and the king took his place on the throne.

Ethan looked over his friends. Gerard's right arm hung in a sling. A bandage covered a wound on his head. Kenneth seemed mostly unscathed. A cut on his left cheek would certainly leave a scar that would take attention away from the scar on the bridge of his best friend's nose. Kiat Fambre leaned on a crutch.

The king looked at Atherton. The guardian of course had no injuries. Ulysses looked as if he had gone through the worst of the battle. He had cuts on the horse half of his body. Bandages wrapped tightly around his muscled torso. Blood seeped from the wound on his side staining the cloth.

The sight of his generals made Ethan wonder how they had won the battle. He suppressed a chuckle at the sight of the men attempting to bow.

"No, save yourselves the trouble and pain. Don't bow."

He called for chairs to be brought in for them. Once everyone was seated he began with his questions. He addressed his first question to Kiat.

"How is your brother? He took a hard blow from the rider."

"He will live. He is resting right now. The orcs that latched on to him took the brunt of the strike. He said he wants to be ready for when the sorcerer returns," the Tulchin explained.

"Good. I am glad he will be alright." Ethan considered what he wanted to ask next. "Please tell me how War was defeated. I remember being choked and passing out."

Kenneth answered next. "You had picked up the sword. War had stepped on it and broke the blade. I assume you panicked as you blacked out because you just swung uncontrollably. Somehow you managed to get the point of the broken blade under the rider's helmet." Kenneth winced as he shifted in his seat. Perhaps his injuries were more on the inside. "Anyway you shoved the blade up under War's chin."

The king nodded. He locked eyes with Gerard. "How are you holding up?"

"An elf broke my wrist and a couple of orcs tried to rip my arm off to beat me with it. I'll be alright," the captain replied.

Ethan looked to Ulysses. He pointed at the wound on the centaur's side. Blood seemed to spread along the bandage. "Is that going to be alright?"

"Yes, but I may not be much use physically in the near future."

"As long as you are still here." The king flashed a brief grin. A more somber question came to him. "Casualties?"

Kenneth lowered his head. "Too many."

"I lost about half of my warriors," Kiat reported. "With about half of the remaining warriors injured."

"How many can fight?"

"Around two hundred."

Ethan took a deep breath. "How many of our men remain?"

"We have about a thousand left. We also took heavy casualties. We lost about half of our troops to death or injuries. We lost some to desertion. The wounded have been taken to Nain with a good number of troops as escort."

Ethan sighed. "Get some rest. We will all need to be at our best the next time."

The men stood. As they did the alarm bells began to ring.

chapter 35

Ethan stood on the outer wall of Castle Bekah. The alarm bells summoned him when the guards first caught sight of the encroaching army. The king wasted no time in rousing every man who could hold a sword. A few men escorted the women out the rear garden gate. He prayed they escaped unseen into the forest.

A sea of otherworldly creatures approached his home. Armored skeletons, orcs and goblins stood right behind Krollnoss. Trolls and large stone-like creatures made up the next wave of the army. Men, elves and centaurs filled in the rest of the giant army's ranks.

Ethan knew this army had only one purpose. Alaric intended to destroy him. Ethan began to doubt he could be victorious against an army of such vast numbers.

The sorcerer sat on a pale horse at the head of the army. He wore a long, hooded cloak, like what the Najera wore. He left the hood down exposing his head. The large black centaur stood on Krollnoss' left. Death sat on a horse to the sorcerer's right. Krollnoss stopped the column outside of the range of most archers.

Mina stood to Ethan's left. She let out a barely audible whimper as she looked out over the enemy's army. Kenneth appeared on the king's right. He stood silent for several moments. No one inside the castle walls spoke. Ethan turned to his friend. He could see concern in Kenneth's eyes.

Kenneth spoke, "Ulysses is waiting at the main gate with every man capable of fighting. All archers are posted on the walls. Kiat and his elves are in the garden."

Ethan did not answer. He stood quietly and stared at the enemy. He prayed. This army seemed greater than any army he had ever seen before. He struggled to keep hope in his spirit. He had to stay strong for the men. He had to be strong for Mina.

"Elyon has abandoned us," whispered one of the men on the wall.

The king snapped his attention to the man. Ethan realized he contemplated giving up just like the man. Ethan knew better. Elyon had not abandoned them. Ethan knew he had to keep his faith strong. Elyon would bring the victory. No weapon or army formed would stand against him.

"No," he finally spoke.

Mina looked at him confused by his outburst. "No what?" she asked.

"No, Elyon has not abandoned us. He has promised never to abandon us," the king said.

The soldier apparently emboldened by the dire circumstances replied, "It looks like He has abandoned us to your enemies."

"Because you look with the wrong eyes," the king said calmly.

The man turned to the soldier next to him. "We should have left with the others."

"Perhaps you should have," Kenneth said.

A sneer crossed the man's face. He raised his voice for as many of the others to hear as possible. "Maybe we should throw the king over so he can take a closer look at what is coming."

Kenneth drew his sword. "You can try."

The king gently pushed his friend's blade down. "You do not have to try." Ethan looked Kenneth in the eye. "Ready my horse."

"You can't go out there," Kenneth protested.

"Just ready my horse." Kenneth bowed his head, turned and pushed men aside to follow the order as quickly as possible. The king turned back to the soldier. "Watch and see Elyon bring the victory today. For your unbelief it will be the last thing you see."

His men parted to create a path as the king passed them on his way to the main gate. Mina followed close behind him protesting the entire way. He heard her words but chose not to respond to any of them. Murmurs rumbled through the gathered men as word spread that the king decided to face the surrounding army alone.

240

Kenneth met Ethan with two horses.

"No," Ethan said sensing his friend's intention.

"You are not going alone," Kenneth said.

Atherton and the centaur joined them. "He must," the guardian said.

Kenneth glared at Atherton. "Stay out of this."

King Ethan placed a hand on his friend's shoulder. "I have to go. Elyon will win the battle. He always has."

"I can't let you go by yourself. You are more than my friend. You are my brother. If you go out there I am going out there too."

"You are my brother, but I have to do this alone."

"You can't fight Krollnoss. He has the power of the Najera and you only have the remainder of the broken sword."

Ethan lifted his hand from Kenneth's shoulder and gave a short wave to cut him off.

"Elyon is with me so no weapon can destroy me. Have faith, my friend."

Kenneth backed away and handed over the reins to the horse. The king accepted the leather straps from his friend.

He turned to Mina. The tears poured down her face in sheets like water cascading over a cliff. He wiped her face with his free hand and then kissed her gently. He knew what she thought and pressed his forehead to hers. "I love you," he told her.

Without another word to anyone he mounted his horse. The king nodded and the gate slowly opened. Ethan took a deep breath. "Close the gate behind me." He spurred his horse forward as he tried to keep his thoughts reassuring.

Elyon would win the day.

Outside the walls Ethan still felt confident in his words
to his men. When he heard the sound of the gate closing
behind him, doubt slowly crept into the edges of his mind.
Alaric rode out to meet the king.

"So, Lyons, have you come to surrender?" Krollnoss
asked.

"No, I came to give *you* that opportunity." Ethan tried to
project the confidence he had before the castle gates closed.

The sorcerer laughed. "I hold control of the larger army.
Why should I give up?"

"Elyon fights for me," Ethan said. He made the
statement simple. No embellishment needed.

The sorcerer turned his horse and returned to his
position next to the last black rider. "Beserth take his head."

The large centaur remained stone faced as he drew the
two handed broadsword from the sheath on his hip. The size
of the blade intimidated Ethan. Doubt now spread like an out
of control fire in his mind and spirit. He looked at the centaur
and then at the centaur's blade again. Ethan believed he was
outmatched.

He saw the other's blade come at his head, just in time
to duck. However he did not see the large fist swinging back at
him from the other direction. With one backhanded slap,
Beserth knocked the king off of his horse.

Ethan lay on his back looking up at the sky. His head
throbbed and cheek burned after the strike. He caught his
breath and realized the centaur wanted to play with him the
way a cat would a cornered mouse. Ethan drew his sword
before sitting up.

When his stalker approached, the king thrust his sword into the horse end of the centaur. No real damage resulted. Beserth did let out a noise that indicated pain but he pulled Ethan's sword from his hide like a splinter. The centaur tossed the weapon aside.

Ethan realized his attack only angered the centaur. Then he noticed a weapon on the ground. He rolled to the weapon and barely avoided being trampled by Beserth's hooves. Ethan jumped to his feet. It took all of the strength he could muster to raise the hammer that fell from the belt of his adversary.

He swung it around and clipped Beserth's left foreleg. Snap! Everyone heard the leg break. The mighty centaur screamed in agony and fell to the ground. The king dropped the hammer by the centaur's side. He intended to show mercy to the creature who had shown none to so many in the past.

"Peace, Beserth," he told his injured opponent who despite the pain and clear tactical disadvantage continued to reach for him. Anger had replaced the look of pain on his face.

"I can heal you through Elyon's power, if you let me."

The centaur only growled his response. Ethan calmly waved a hand and the centaur seemed to pass out. Ethan began to turn his attention to the sorcerer and ducked at the sound of arrows flying through the air. He turned to see Kenneth on top of the wall, bow in hand.

The king turned and looked toward his enemy. A pair of orcs lay dead midway between he and the sorcerer. Ethan watched for Krollnoss to make his next move. Krollnoss sat on his horse and pressed his lips together as he glared at Ethan. He was sure the sorcerer was angry but could not tell if he was more angry at Ethan or the centaur. Ethan decided he could not wait for Krollnoss to make his next move. He had to take action and go on the offensive.

chapter 36

Alaric snarled. His anger grew from wrath to rage. Beserth was supposed to be one of the best soldiers money could buy. He had paid the centaur a lot of gold and silver for his services. Beserth would pay for his failure. Alaric decided to punish him later. Lyons stood boldly on the opposite side of the battlefield.

"I challenge you, sorcerer. Face me as champion of your army!" the king yelled.

Alaric grinned, he had no intention of fighting Lyons. The reason he desired the medallion and power over the Najera was simply to control the army. He raised his left hand. Only one word came out of his mouth in response to the king's challenge.

"Attack!" He threw his raised hand forward.

Nothing moved. The elves, centaurs and men Beserth brought with him did not raise a weapon. The supernatural armies of the Najera remained still and quiet. The orcs stood as statues. The only movement came in the form of a giant shadow that circled the battlefield.

Alaric lifted his eyes to the sky. A large, black dragon flew around in a continuous circle. The creature was like a vulture waiting to pick the bones of the dead. No animals cried out. The wind refused to blow. The only sound that could be heard over the battlefield was the occasional whoosh of the dragon's wings.

The sorcerer looked back at his army in bewilderment. He clutched the medallion. He controlled the armies of the Najera. He looked back at Death without a word.

Why do they not obey me?

"Because you have not answered the challenge put forth to you," said the wild haired prophet. He always appeared as if from nowhere.

The prophet's answer astonished the sorcerer. The old man had read his thoughts. The prophet stood there in his outdated robes with that disgusting cheerful grin on his face. Alaric wondered why he was always so cheery. Especially now when his king was about to die.

"As you can see, your king has already defeated my best warrior," Alaric said from his horse. He motioned with is hand at the centaur who lay at Ethan's feet.

The prophet looked at the unconscious warrior. "Really? He was your best?"

Alaric recognized the old man's attempt to turn his army against him. "Of course he was."

"With all of the power under your control he was your greatest warrior? Your champion?" the prophet said.

Alaric glared at Lyons. He stood tall and defiant, sword in hand with no expression on his face. He glanced back at the Najera.

"You do control the strength and weapon prowess of War," the hooded skeleton stated with a hiss.

The sorcerer turned back to his enemy. He suspected Lyons and the prophet were stalling and laying a trap for him. Alaric looked all around. He saw no movement on the battlefield other than the shadow of the dragon. Still he did not want to take any chances and barked orders for the elves to keep alert.

"You didn't answer me, Alaric," the prophet said. "With all of the power you control, you say this centaur is your champion? Or are you willing to personally answer the challenge. After all here stands the King of Eden and Warrior of Elyon. He is his own champion.

"And if I insist that the centaur is my champion?"

"Then you are defeated," the prophet said with the silly half grin. "Surrender the medallion."

Alaric became disgusted at himself. He walked into a trap after all. It was not the kind of trap he expected. He kicked the flanks of his horse to move the animal forward. He stared at the prophet and smiled.

"Well played, old man."

The prophet's lips moved but the sorcerer did not hear what the man said. He only heard the rattle of his armor as he dismounted and the labored breathing from Beserth. The shadow circled again. The dragon continued its vigil around them.

Alaric stopped next to his former lieutenant. The hammer of the rider known as War appeared in his hand at will. He enjoyed this power. He would enjoy killing Lyons too. He rested the head of the long hammer on the ground and stood over the broken centaur. One hand remained on the handle and each foot posted on either side of his prey.

Beserth begged for mercy. The sorcerer made no effort to reach for the centaur. He only bent forward slightly. "I cannot reward your failure again."

He grabbed the handle of the weapon with both hands. He raised it up and quickly brought it down onto the other's head. Everyone heard the crunch as Beserth's skull fractured and the crack as his neck broke.

Alaric then looked back at the prophet. The old man no longer stood on the battlefield. Only King Lyons. "I'll deal with you in a moment."

Lyons did not move.

The sorcerer turned his attention to the sky.

"Now for you," he said knowing the winged reptile would not hear him.

A bow and arrow replaced the hammer in his hand. He drew back the arrow and took aim at the dragon. Someone shouted out a name. Alaric released the arrow but the dragon easily dodged the projectile. It veered off toward the rear of the castle. Alaric looked back a Lyons. The bow became the hammer again. He stormed toward his enemy.

"Prepare to die!"

chapter 37

The sorcerer's execution of Beserth revolted Ethan. The action did not surprise him but disgusted him nonetheless. Ethan was glad to see that Kyros, the dragon king, came to help but was more happy to see that the arrow from the sorcerer missed the dragon.

Now the sorcerer turned his hate filled gaze to the king. Ethan raised his sword, ready to defend himself. He steadied himself and hoped Elyon would once again win the day for him. Alaric swung the mighty hammer.

Ethan jumped back to avoid the blow but had to keep moving away as the sorcerer continued to swing the weapon at him. Alaric's attacks were swift and fluid. He used the head and the handle of the hammer to come at Ethan. The large hammer floated around the sorcerer's body. In a lethal display of strength and grace.

Alaric had moved in close enough for the shaft of the hammer to clang against Ethan's sword. The king's weapon was torn from his hand. He continued to dodge the hammer until he stood only a few feet from the castle wall. Krollnoss grinned his toothy wicked grin. It was the same look that his brother, Xestes, would give to Ethan. The king hated seeing that grin on Xestes' face and hated it more now because of everything Alaric had done to his kingdom.

Ethan started to lose his focus. If he did that he would surely die out here today. The sorcerer pulled the war hammer up and over his head. He delivered an overhand strike. The head of the hammer crashed into the ground as the king quickly spun out of the way.

Ethan took two quick steps forward and drew his first back and leapt into the air toward his opponent. He launched his fist mid-air. The punch landed on the sorcerer's mouth.

A stunned Alaric released the war hammer and stumbled backward. He wiped blood from his lips and grinned again. He seemed to enjoy the fight. He charged Ethan.

The king braced to defend himself. Alaric wrapped his arms around Ethan. With one arm now pinned at his side the king struggled to break his opponent's grip. Alaric lifted the king off of the ground. Ethan tried to slam his free hand into the side of his captor's head.

Unfazed the sorcerer rushed forward with the king still in his arms. Ethan slammed against the stone wall with a thud. All of his breath rushed out and for a moment refused to return. Alaric released him.

The king slid down the wall trying to breathe again. Breath returned to him after a moment or two of trying. Alaric grabbed his prey by the hair and dragged him to his feet. He pulled the king toward him and drove his knee into Ethan's mid-section.

After several knees to the stomach he tossed the king to the ground.

He's toying with you. He knows as well as you do without the Najera weapons, you cannot win.

Ethan pushed himself up to his hands and knees. He felt two quick kicks in the ribs. He heard the crack and felt rib break at the same time.

"I've failed you, Elyon," Ethan whispered.

Another kick pounded into his side. The king collapsed. He lay on the ground and knew he was seriously injured. He coughed and blood dribbled down his chin. Pain shot through his sides as he struggled to get to his feet. Alaric arrogantly strutted to him. Ethan made it to his knees.

The sorcerer struck with a front kick toward Ethan's face. The king batted the other's foot away but he could not block the second kick. He fell to his back. The king released a moan and closed his eyes.

He heard a soft voice whisper to him. It was a voice he had heard in the past. Elyon spoke to him.

"You are my Warrior. Your feet are shod by my peace."

"Elyon?" the king whispered.

"You wear my truth around your waist. My righteousness is in your heart. My salvation covers you."

The words settled his spirit. His limbs felt warm and energized. Courage dispelled the fear and doubt that now gripped his heart. Armor appeared as the voice continued, though he was unsure if he even had the strength to stand in it.

"I don't think—," Ethan started.

The voice cut him off.

"Your faith in me is your shield. My words are your sword."

Ethan's sword jumped back to his hand and a small shield appeared in the other. He began to protest again but only sighed.

The voice spoke again only louder. Ethan opened his eyes. It seemed only he was able to hear the voice.

"If I stand with you nothing can stand against you. No weapon created can harm you."

"I don't have the strength to fight anymore, master."

"You don't fight with your strength. You don't fight by your might but by my spirit says your Lord!"

Suddenly Ethan felt strength return to him. The armor rattled as he stood. Alaric's wicked grin disappeared. The sorcerer charged in with a strong left punch. The king raised his shield and blocked the blow.

Alaric shook his hand and reached toward the war hammer. The weapon flew through the air to his hand just like Ethan's had. He began another combination of graceful twirls that ended with an overhand strike on the king's shield. Under normal circumstances the shield would have broken after such an attack. Ethan's shield held strong.

The hammer head crumbled to the ground. The king began his attack. He swung his sword in three swift strikes. Each attack from a different angle. Alaric blocked each strike with the long headless shaft of the war hammer. The fury of the king's attacks drove the sorcerer to one knee. Ethan let loose with an overhand slice of his sword that cut through the war hammer's handle.

The king easily blocked the sorcerer's feeble efforts to hit him with the remains of the the war hammer shaft. Krollnoss dropped the pieces of the handle and stood. With a slight jump and a front kick, Ethan placed the flat of his boot in the chest of his enemy. Krollnoss fell on his back.

The sorcerer stood and a sword appeared in his right hand. With a swift cut Ethan removed the hand from its owner. Gauntlet, hand and sword fell to the ground. Alaric's eyes flitted back and forth between the bleeding stump where his hand used to be to the hand that still gripped the sword where it lay on the ground.

Stunned Alaric dropped to his knees. He had been defeated. Even controlling the power of the Najera he could not defeat the Warrior of Elyon. He waited for the death stroke to fall but it did not come.

King Lyons spoke but Alaric did not hear the words only the tone of the voice. The king had removed his helmet. The sorcerer realized he would likely die because of his wound but he could still win. He controlled the power of death.

Alaric stood and walked toward the king. He called for the final rider. Death dismounted. It walked with confident strides toward the two men. Alaric's own steps were not as quick as usual but they had purpose.

They reached Lyons at the same moment. The king made no attempt to run or even defend himself. Alaric smiled, he would win.

"Finish him," he commanded the Najera.

The creature pulled back the black hood on the cloak that covered its skinless head.

"No," it said.

The creature bent over and picked up the sorcerer's severed hand. It pried the sword from the fingers of the gauntlet and tossed the hand away. Alaric lifted the medallion from off of his chest.

"I control you, remember."

"No. You don't. You control the armies of the other three riders, when you have proven yourself worthy of them."

"You are breaking our agreement?"

Death shook its head. "No. There never was an agreement made. You did not sacrifice what you held most dear." The creature slowly stalked the sorcerer much like he had done to many of an enemy in the past.

"My brother—,"

"No, Alaric, your brothers never meant much to you. Power is what you cared about. *Your* power."

Anger took control of Alaric. He punched the creature in the face with his good hand. The skeleton rider's lower jaw became dislocated.

The rider raised one boney hand and put the jaw bone back in its place. The Najera just cackled. Alaric's hand began to warm. A moment later it burned and began to blacken as if being consumed by invisible flames. He fell to the ground screaming and writhing in pain.

The Najera stood over him. "You did not sacrifice what meant the most to you. You gave me your brother. You should have given me *your* life."

It took the sword and pointed the tip to Alaric's chest. It pushed the blade down but the sorcerer barely felt the weapon pierce his chest. The pain in his left hand and arm ceased. He saw Death pull the sword up. It bent over and a bony hand grabbed the medallion.

"No man has power over death."

Another cackle sounded but Alaric barely heard it. His vision darkened. A cold chill rushed through his body. He released a final breath and was no more.

Chapter 38

Ethan watched as Krollnoss took his final breath. He did not know why he made no effort to stop the Najera. The sorcerer was his enemy but as a Warrior of Elyon, Ethan knew he had an obligation to protect everyone. Even those who did not deserve that protection. The king realized he did not have any more time to dwell on it as the final Najera turned to him. Ethan jumped back, sword drawn and ready to fight.

"Give up. You cannot defeat me now," it said. Death cackled again. It slipped the chain around its head. The medallion dropped onto its chest and seemed to glow.

Ethan struck first. He swung his sword at the rider's head but missed. Death blocked and parried the next several attacks. Pain cut through his side again. Each swing he took drained the breath from him.

Death took the offensive. Ethan stepped back with each blow that clanged against his sword or his armor. Death kicked Ethan in the chest forcing the king back into the castle wall and stopping the king's retreat. Death's next strike sent the king to his knees. He dropped his sword. Ethan dropped down to his hands and knees painfully trying to catch his breath.

Icy fingers gripped the back of his neck. Death yanked the king to his feet. Ethan wobbled a little before regaining his balance. The rider's dark and empty eye sockets chilled Ethan. He had failed. Death controlled the medallion. The Najera would sweep across all of the kingdoms destroying all it saw.

"For centuries men have sought to defeat me. Even when I was locked in that prison death is the only force to which man could never conquer. Men can overcome famine, fear and even war if they so choose. They cannot overcome death. Every man, woman and child is destined to face me."

Ethan rasped trying to respond to the rider's statement. The rider grabbed the front of Ethan's throat and squeezed. It lifted Ethan off of the ground and pulled him closer to its face.

"Every Warrior of Elyon has met the same fate whether they have faced me in battle or not. They are all dead. It is your time to join them."

Death pulled the king forward and thrust the sword into Ethan at the same time.

Kenneth stood on the wall and watched the battles below. His friend looked to have lost against the centaur but somehow he found a way to overcome Beserth. When Krollnoss attacked Ethan defeated him as well. As long as they have been fighting together, Kenneth had always witnessed his friend end the battle as the ultimate victor.

Together they had fought battles against enemies one on one. They had been outnumbered thousands to one when he and Ethan and their other friends defeated Alaric's brother, Xestes. Kenneth could not believe his eyes.

He watched as Alaric died and the rider slipped the sword out of his chest like a cook had just carved into a side of beef. Kenneth could tell that Ethan was losing his strength. He worried for his friend. For the second time in just a few weeks, Kenneth felt useless.

He watched as each strike that Ethan either made or absorbed seemed to weaken him. Kenneth silently prayed. Elyon had to win the battle. He had to save his friend.

Please, Elyon do something, Kenneth prayed.

Mina slid up next to him and wrapped her arms around him. Kenneth recognized the fear in her face. He felt the same fear. Kenneth did not want to lose his friend. More importantly Ethan was the last hope for anyone to stop the Najera.

Kenneth put his arm around Mina to try to reassure her that everything would be alright. He tried to assure himself as well. He squeezed her gently. He watched Ethan on his hands and knees. Death picked him up by his neck and set his friend on his feet. From his spot on the wall he could not hear the words the rider spoke to Ethan but knew they could not be good.

Next to him he felt Mina hold her breath then realized he was not breathing either. He released his breath. The blade of Death's sword punched through Ethan's back. Mina yelped and buried her face in Kenneth's shoulder. Kenneth's knees wobbled and a shudder went through his body.

Kenneth had to hold Mina on her feet as she sobbed uncontrollably. He fought against the urge to break down in tears himself. Death looked up at him as he pushed Ethan's body off of the blade. The men on the wall began to murmur and panic at the sight of their king falling to the ground.

chapter 39

Slowly Ethan opened his eyes. He blinked several times at the onslaught of light that filled them. A hand reached out for him. Blindly he grabbed the hand and felt himself being pulled to his feet. His eyes refocused and he recognized the faces that surrounded him.

They were not the faces he thought he would see. He saw his father, his uncle and Meldorn. He blurted out his question before even thinking about it.

"Am I dead?"

His uncle spoke. "No. Not yet."

"Then what...what is this?"

"A vision," Meldorn answered.

Ethan looked to his father. "I have failed to protect the kingdom, Father."

King Drew smiled. "You have not failed yet. There is still time."

"But—,"

"Remember," the father continued ignoring his son's protest. "I am proud of who you have turned out to be."

Ethan shook his head. "How can I defeat death? All men must die. There is nothing that I can do."

"Of course not," Rufus said. His uncle had always spoken in riddles when he wanted Ethan to learn something profound about Elyon. The prophet and Meldorn, both did the same. Perhaps that is the reason Ethan had felt such a connection to the Rathuan.

"I don't understand. How can I stop the rider from destroying the world?"

"You can't win in a fight against death. No man can beat death," Rufus said.

Ethan felt angry and confused. He felt he would be better off just giving up and letting Death take him. He would join Elyon in paradise and not have the worries of being king to care about any longer. Then he thought of Mina and Kenneth. He could not leave them on their own to face this creature.

Pain pierced his chest. More time passed between each breath. The pain intensified with each breath he took. Ethan tried to focus but knew his time was getting short. Either his vision would end or his life would.

Finally Meldorn spoke. "What your uncle means is that in your own power you cannot defeat death. You must rely on Elyon. Only He can overcome death."

The king screamed and dropped to his knees. He looked up to the faces of the men he had just been speaking to. They simply faded away. Another pain ran from his chest through his body. He closed his eyes and collapsed.

When he opened his eyes again, Ethan blinked a couple of times to clear his vision. Cold, damp dirt pressed against his cheek. The smell of grass filled his nose. He was alive. His father was right. He still had time.

Pain tore through his chest. He could not ignore the wound. "Elyon," he called out with his face still in the dirt.

From his place on the grass the king heard the cheers from the army in front of him. He recognized the warmth that coursed through his body as Elyon's strength. Slowly he stood bracing himself with the castle wall.

When he was on his feet he watched Death face its terrible army with its hands in the air and the sword raised high in victory. The creature turned as if to address those in the castle.

The bony jaw dropped and the mouth gaped open. For only a moment Ethan imagined what Death's face looked like if it were covered with muscle and skin. He saw eyes widened by a raised brow and stretched lips surrounding the opened mouth. The king dismissed the image and readied himself for the final fight.

"Elyon please finish this."

The king reached his hands out for his sword and shield. The weapons leapt to his hands just as they had before. He tightened his grip on his sword.

"Every man must die," he said. "But Elyon holds the ultimate power over life and death."

He paused for a breath that still shot pain through his chest but not to the extent it hurt before. "You are right, rider, one day I will die. It will be when Elyon chooses. It will not be this day. It will not be by your hand."

The rider released a roar of fury. Ethan ran forward with all he had left in him. He knew Elyon pumped his arms and legs and because he could not remember a time when he had run so fast.

The king jumped a few steps in front of the rider. His shield arm coiled back and thrust forward like a viper striking its prey as he landed. The edge of his shield struck the Najera's forehead.

The rider staggered back. A thick, black liquid oozed from the fracture left by the blow. The king smelled the rotten stench of decay. The odor made him want to vomit. He forced himself to continue the fight.

Ethan raised his sword and spun around one time to build momentum. He brought his blade around. The rider raised its own sword to parry the incoming attack.

The rider's sword broke in half as the king's blade crashed into it. Ethan finished the arc by cutting through the bones of the rider's neck.

Both the king and the skeletal body of the rider fell to the ground. Ethan pushed himself to his knees. He watched the Najera's skull stop rolling a few feet away. A black mist swirled as the remains of the last Najera disappeared. Like the other riders the black mist was drawn into the medallion.

The king picked up the medallion. His mission was complete. Now he felt he could die in peace. He felt his strength drain from him. A scream came from the wall. A man's terrified voice yelled out that he could not see.

"Elyon have mercy on the man I cursed. Please return his sight in three days." Ethan prayed.

Ethan's eyes closed and he fell forward to the ground.

chapter 40

Ethan awoke in what had become a familiar manner. He was not sure where he was or even if he was in the world of the living or the dead.

A cough escaped his mouth and he winced with the pain in his chest. Another cough and another shot of pain told him that Elyon kept him alive. He closed his eyes and tried to relax.

"My Lady, the king is awake!" shouted a woman. The owner of the voice ran out of the room shouting down the hall.

Ethan tried to adjust himself to be more comfortable. Mina rushed into the room and to his side. She plopped down on the side of the bed and wrapped her arms around his neck. She kissed him like she had not seen him in years.

She ended the kiss and placed her forehead against his. "I thought I had lost you," she whispered. Lines of tears poured from her eyes.

His personal surgeon entered the room next. The old man shooed Mina away so he could examine the king. Mina and the servants swiftly took left the old man to his work. After a few minutes he declared that the king was healing well.

"Only Elyon could have kept you alive after the beating you took."

"That's one more thing I need to thank Him for." The old man smiled and walked out of the door.

Kenneth, Mina and the prophet entered the room after the surgeon granted them permission. Mina took her place at his side again.

"How are you feeling?" Kenneth asked.

"I am tired of waking up in bed feeling like I had been trampled by a family of dragons."

"Well you look better than you feel then," Kenneth said with his crooked toothed grin.

"As long as I look like me again," the king said trying to return his friend's smile.

"Yes, except for a few bruises you look like your handsome self again." Mina said. "Finally. It was so hard seeing your face on that man."

The king looked at the three faces and smiled weakly. "Where is the medallion?"

The prophet raised his arm, the medallion dropped from his hand and dangled on the chain.

"How do we destroy it?" Kenneth asked.

"We will speak about that journey at another time after you have recovered sufficiently. For now I will keep the medallion. I will take my leave now, majesty. I think the three of you need to speak among yourselves for a while. I am sure you have questions. We will have other matters to speak of soon enough."

The prophet turned and left the trio of friends.

No one spoke for a moment. The king winced again with another deep breath. "Where is Ulysses and Kiat?"

"Ulysses decided he would personally go to Tilibra and help Gerard move his wife to Eden," Kenneth answered.

"Gerard is to retain his rank as captain and will join my personal guard." Kenneth nodded his acknowledgement.

Mina stroked Ethan's forehead. "Kiat returned home to his family."

"They deserve some time together. We will give them a couple of weeks and then make an official visit to grant medals to him and his people for valor."

Ethan shifted again. He took a deep breath. The pain was not as intense this time. He took Mina's hand and kissed the top. The king looked at his friend.

"How's Krysta and the baby?"

"They are good. They arrived this morning."

"Good. Can I have some time with Mina?"

"Of course. You need to know King Maras is here. He arrived yesterday," Kenneth said. "He is waiting for a meeting with you."

"Yesterday? How long have I been sleeping?"

"Three days," Mina said.

"Three days?" She nodded.

Ethan flipped his blanket up and moved to swing his legs over the side of the bed.

"What are you doing?" Mina demanded.

Pain shot through his torso. Ethan closed his eyes and leaned back on the bed. "I have to meet with King Maras."

"No, he can wait. You need more rest."

"I need to move."

Mina glared at him. He knew how serious she was.

He looked at Kenneth. "Inform the king I will meet him in two hours. Then send me some food and water for a bath." He shifted again. "And a couple of servants to assist me."

Mina's glare softened. "Fine." She stood, leaned over and kissed him and then exited the room.

After his meal and bath he found the strength to dress. Carefully he took each step down the staircase and into the throne room. He sat down on his throne.

The king and queen of Tilibra entered followed closely by their daughter, Amber who smiled shyly at Ethan. The seemed taken back by his appearance.

"I look worse than I feel, I assure you," Ethan said.

"We are supposed to have an audience with the king," Vincent Maras said.

Ethan slowly nodded. "When you saw me last I was under the spell of the sorcerer. This is my true face."

King Maras seemed to relax. Amber's admiration seemed to grow at learning she saw his true face. He felt his cheeks get hot. A sideways glance at Mina told him she saw Amber's look as well. Mina did not hide her anger.

"King Maras, welcome to my home. I apologize for the delay in this meeting."

"No apology necessary, majesty. I understand you were recovering from your injuries."

Ethan caught Amber's eye. He recognized the look of a woman in love. He remembered the same look from Mina years ago when she first fell in love with him. Mina's scowl had grown scarier. She obviously had seen the look on Amber's face as well. Her eyes pierced deep into his skull, like there was something he could have done to stop the way Amber felt.

Ethan thought the best that he could do was change the subject.

"King Vincent, what can I do for you?"

King Maras bowed his head slightly and pursed his lips together. He appeared remorseful. He raised his head and knelt.

"Majesty, I am truly sorry for not coming to your aid before. You saved my kingdom, my daughter and essentially the world. Captain Casser was right. I owe you everything. I am here to pledge my allegiance to you. If there is ever anything your kingdom is in need of, just ask."

"I appreciate the declaration and know that if there is anything you and your kingdom needs, Eden will stand with you."

King Maras stood. "Thank you. In order to seal the our pledges I have a proposal. I offer you the hand of my daughter in marriage."

Ethan closed his eyes. This was not the change he hoped for. Amber's face lit up. Ethan could not be sure but thought he heard a growl come from Mina's direction. He dared not look at her at this time.

His mind raced for words as fast as his heart pounded against his ribs. He knew he should speak but the words would not form. From the corner of his eye he saw Mina begin to storm away. She huffed with each step.

Her action caused the words to come. He lifted his chin to signal for Kenneth to stop her. Ethan looked King Maras in the eye.

"Your proposal is a generous one. I have no doubt that Princess Amber would be a most excellent queen." Ethan looked at Amber. He could already see the tears form in her eyes.

"She will be a fantastic queen," King Maras said with a look of pride. His wife seemed to sense what Ethan had to say. She placed a hand on her daughter's shoulder.

"The position of Queen of Eden was promised to another a long time ago."

Ethan turned to face Mina. Slowly she turned to look at him. Ethan stood. With each step his body ached as he descended the steps from his throne. He walked to her and took her hands in his.

"That is if you will still be my wife," he whispered.

Tears filled her eyes. "Yes."

Ethan turned back to King Maras. Amber buried her face into her mother's shoulder. Ethan's stomach turned at the thought of hurting the young woman.

"I am sorry. I mean no offense and hope your family will forgive me."

King Maras gave a slight smile. "No offense taken. I understand. Let me be the first to congratulate you."

The King of Tilibra joined Ethan and Mina. He stuck out a hand. Ethan accepted it and they shook.

The prophet finally spoke. "I sensed I would be needed."

"What, now?" Ethan asked.

Mina smiled. "Why not?"

Ethan did not want to be cruel to Amber. "You don't want a fancy wedding."

"Everyone is already here who is important. I don't need a fancy wedding," Mina said. She could not stop smiling.

"What about Ulysses? He's not here."

Kenneth raised one hand. The other now held Krysta's free hand. Olin lay silently in her other arm. "Ulysses doesn't like weddings. Remember, he visited his family during ours."

Ethan glanced at Queen Maras. She had a soft smile on her face. Amber had stopped crying. The queen softly stroked her daughter's head and nodded to Ethan.

"Very well, prophet. Go ahead," Ethan said.

The prophet began to speak on the importance of the commitment between a husband and wife. After a few moments of explanation he looked at Ethan. "Majesty, will take this woman as your wife?"

"I will."

The prophet looked at Mina. "Will you take King Ethan as your husband?"

"I will," she answered.

"Then it is my pleasure to proclaim that you are now husband and wife."

Ethan leaned in and kissed his queen. She wrapped her arms around his neck and kissed him back. Ethan pulled away as the people gathered around them cheered and clapped.

For the first time in years, Ethan fully felt at peace.

The End

ABOUT THE AUTHOR

Aaron began his writing career in church writing sketches, plays and stories for Sunday school, Christmas and other occasions. He is a fan of fantasy and science fiction novels and movies. *The Honor of Elyon* is his fourth novel. Aaron currently lives in Southeast Michigan with his wife and son.

Coming Soon
From the Desk of
Aaron W. Baldwin

The Black Wolf

Half elf, half human, Bane grew up unwanted by both societies. After his mother is murdered during a raid by elves, Bane is taken to live among them. He is trained as a warrior and quickly rises through the ranks to become an elite assassin.

When Bane is given an assigned to take a life that he cannot force himself to take he finds himself again in exile. Only this time he is hunted by the only assassin able to take him out.

After saving the life of a boy in the forest, Bane reluctantly becomes the protector of the boy and his mother while escorting them to the city of the gods.

Fighting the memories of his past, his station in society as a half-breed and his hunter, Bane's task is difficult enough. When the boy's mother learns of her protector's past Bane's mission becomes more life and death than either of them can know.

Life On The Run

Shane Clayton flew to Hawaii to celebrate getting married to the woman of his dreams. The only problem, his bride to be left him at the alter for the co-star of his poorly rated sitcom.

After having one too man drinks on the plane he wakes up in his hotel suite with a women claiming to be a federal agent, a folder full of graffiti covered head shots of his former love and a bad headache.

Shane becomes wrapped up in this woman's crusade to stop an arms dealer she believes killed her brother. Shane realizes too late that he is in too deep and may have to spend the rest of his life running from the government.